A VARIETY OF WEAPONS

THE LT. VALCOUR SERIES

Murder by the Clock
Somewhere in This House
Murder by Latitude
Murder in the Willet Family
Murder on the Yacht
Valcour Meets Murder
The Lesser Antilles Case
Profile of a Murder
The Case of the Constant God
Crime of Violence
Murder Masks Miami

OTHER MYSTERIES

The Case of the Dowager's Etchings
The Case of the Redoubled Cross
The Deadly Dove
Design in Evil
Diagnosis Murder
Duenna to a Murder
The Faces of Danger
The Lethal Lady
Murder De Luxe
Museum Piece No 13
Murder de Luxe
The Steps to Murder
A Variety of Weapons
A Woman is Dead

SCIENCE FICTION

The Fatal Kiss Mystery

DOG STORIES

North Star: A Dog Story of the Northwest
Whelp of the Winds: A Dog Story

A VARIETY OF WEAPONS

RUFUS KING

WILDSIDE PRESS

Published by Wildside Press LLC
www.wildsidepress.com

CHAPTER I

Sun sliced in with elegance through slatted blinds while New York sweltered far below, and Fanny Mistral, Inc., thought: Of all damn days for ocelots!

She was a tightened woman, like a very smart and newly reupholstered chair, unyielding, exact, and, as with most career women, electric with charm, with a swift awareness of the least happenings in her celebrated world, and frightened stiff of common human warmth.

Fanny lifted an office telephone and said: "Ask Miss Ledrick to come in, please."

She thought, while waiting, of Ann Ledrick and on the general oddity of how chance could type you for life. Several months ago Fanny had sent for Ann simply because the girl had won an award in the *Year Book of American Photography* for a stunning shot of a Manx cat: fast pan, 1/100 sec., f:22. She had looked at Ann's other stuff: more cats, many dogs, that handsome thing of a colt in sun-tipped wheat, then those frustrated eyes of a tiger in the Bronx Zoo. She had hired Ann on the spot.

The bulk of Fanny's prominent clients owned pets, and there had been no one in the office who had ever touched Ann Ledrick's work. Victor Lejeune was the nearest, but he remained far better with dowagers whose bosoms he could reduce through his artistry in lighting and with capitalistic giants whom he succeeded in keeping titanic while rendering them less harassed (he did something with a spot which neutralized the suicidal gleam), but with animals his portraits had always registered a reproachful reaction of outraged distaste.

Fanny looked up as Ann Ledrick came in, and for a moment the warmth of a human doubt made her wonder: Is it fair? I don't quite like this. The ocelots won't be bad, but there's the whole unpleasant atmosphere of the job. When you thought what the place must be like even after twenty years. Its atmosphere would not have dissipated from the very fact that Marlow would have kept it alive: brooding in it, steeped in it as he was reputed to have been throughout those two decades. No matter with what luxury and truffled wealth.

Not that there could be any danger in a physical sense, unless you considered the imponderables of a mind so inbred with the companionship of tragedy and hate—hate? Yes, Fanny thought, that would be there too: a hatred against a social structure that for twenty years had turned a deaf ear to Marlow's lone, pitiable cry and made it impotent. Absurd. Anecdotes concerning a place of that sort were always fantastic. It was the same way with that stupendous ranch in Texas where men were rumored to have entered and never to have been seen again. The tepid warmth cooled, and Fanny was efficiently electric again.

"Sit down, Miss Ledrick."

"Thank you."

"You are leaving for Black Tor at three this afternoon from the airport. A Marlow plane will take you. They have their own landing field on the grounds which are, incidentally, four thousand acres in the heart of the Adirondacks. There is a common rumor that entire safaris have perished from starvation while attempting to trek to the house itself. A rumor highly discouraging to uninvited guests, especially as there are no roads. People simply do not drop in."

"It sounds like the lair of a cult."

"It isn't. I am afraid you will be bored stiff with normality. You will be plied with pressed duck and caviar and with trout so fresh that they still look dazed. Champagne will glitter through you, and you will take a lot of pretty pictures of Estelle Marlow's beloved ocelots. There are three of the brutes, and she obviously adores them because she evacuated them with her from Paris around a year ago. You must tell me, when you get back, how."

"I will. With details of their reception in Lisbon."

"Good. Miss Marlow specified when she telephoned that you be sent. Her cousin remembered your shot of the Manx in the *Year Book* and is still impressed. You know, that's odd—"

"What is?"

"How did Marlow know you were with us? Certainly not from the *Year Book*. But then it isn't, really."

"Why?"

"People of Marlow's wealth, Miss Ledrick, just say to their secretary: 'Get me that girl who did the Manx cat.' And you're got. You are expected to stay at Black Tor for a week and perhaps longer."

For a moment Fanny studied Ann critically as a woman and not as a Graflex. It's all right, Fanny thought. The girl is devilishly attractive-looking if you like the dark Irish type, and she has style. She'd never set loose any glares of anguish among the six best-dressed women, but that's only because she hasn't the money to buy the clothes that they can. Certainly she was manner enough, what with Spence and her training in hauling ropes of daisies over the grass at Vassar. Fanny was a little bitter about this. Her own daisy culture had taken place on Grandpa Eulis' farm in Oshkoton, Iowa.

Fanny said, "How are you off for clothes?"

"Better put it down as adequate. Than which there is little grimmer."

"All right. Estelle Marlow suggests something warm. She says it gets cold in the mountains. She must be something of a homebody in spite of her ocelots, although I can't see how." A touch of earthy humanity once more disturbed Fanny. "Do you know about the Marlows?"

"No. Should I?"

"Not necessarily. It was a long time ago."

"What was?"

Fanny said sharply, "Nothing. Nothing that could possibly be of the slightest consequence to anyone today. Justin Marlow is a man in his late seventies. Estelle Marlow is his cousin. She must be in her forties and was one of the sights of Paris until the Germans chased her out. It was a common habit for sight-seeing buses to lump her in with the Arc de Triomphe and Gertrude Stein. Her salon was a feeding trough for battered tiaras and dented crowns. I want a blow-by-blow report on her too."

"What will I need?"

"Your camera, film packs, and flash bulbs. They've everything else there, and she wants the works. Your job is to stay until she gets them. Good-by, Miss Ledrick."

"Good-by."

Fanny found herself watching the closing door. She also found herself shuddering as she muttered, "And good luck."

The telephone was ringing when Ann reached her office. She lifted the receiver, and the pleasant voice of Miss Dingley on the switchboard said, "Mr. Forrest is calling from Washington. Just a minute, please, and I'll put him through."

For the past month, since he had quit his post as general manager in Fanny Mistral, Inc., and had taken over a government job in Washington, Bill Forrest had telephoned Ann at odd times. Some had been a bit too odd, specifically the four-o'clock-in-the-morning ones when Bill said he had been overcome with impulsive insomnia and that nothing but the sound of her voice could put him to sleep.

"Ann?" his voice said.

"Yes, Bill?"

"I'm in a hurry, so get this straight. I've a thousand things to do in nothing flat."

"So have I. I have to leave in an hour and pose ocelots."

"Now listen, Ann—Did you say ocelots?"

"Yes."

"Well, don't bother me with trifles. Just run up to the zoo and do it."

"They're in the Adirondacks."

"Nonsense. I'm getting two weeks' leave starting next Friday and will pick you up in that dear little two-by-four you call home at seven."

"But I won't be there, Bill. I'll be in the heart of the Adirondacks, drinking champagne and posing ocelots."

"Have you gone mad?"

"No, and I'm to be stuffed with pressed duck, caviar, and dazed trout."

"You have gone mad. I can't waste any more time because I've got to clear up my job here and become a marine. They told me this morning they'd let me play. I got sick of sitting on my rump in a chair that doesn't even swivel and have decided to become a hero. So get sane by Friday and I'll pick you up at seven and marry you. Good-by."

The receiver at the Washington end of the conversation went bang.

An hour after Ann had left, Miss Dingley at the switchboard said: "Fanny Mistral, Incorporated. Good afternoon."

"Bill again, Dingley. Put me through to Ann."

"She left. She was due at the airport about ten minutes ago."

"Give me Fanny."

Fanny, who regarded Bill's facade as something more than photogenic, cordially laced her voice with warmth when she answered.

"Bill darling, how are you?"

"I'm fine, but it's not the point. Wasn't it the Marlow woman, the dopey cousin in Paris, who landed here last fall and got the press about her ocelots?"

"Yes, dear. They had a suite on A Deck while the rest of the cabins were crushed with vertical diplomats."

"I knew it. I realized it about two minutes ago. And you've sent Ann up to Black Tor in the Adirondacks?"

"Yes, darling."

"Alone?"

"*Yes*, darling."

"Well, I'll be damned!"

Bang.

CHAPTER II

A victoria with a pair of stunning bays was waiting at the Black Tor airfield.

There had been little conversation on the plane beyond a few conventionalities offered by Ann to the pilot, who had struck her as being very old and very tired. She had put him down (correctly) as a contemporary of the Wright brothers.

Also, thoughts of Bill had occupied her. Today was Saturday, and next Friday at seven he would show up and marry her. Just breeze in and whisk her away from her packing-box nest on East Thirty-sixth Street and haul her by her raven tresses off to Elkton, or wherever it was that justices of the peace performed such enduring ceremonies with a snap.

Yes, he would.

She had muttered this phrase about seven times before she caught the pilot glancing at her with something more than polite curiosity.

All right, her muttering mind had run on, Bill has left a good, safe, and important job in Washington and signed up with the Marines. So off to Montezuma, with the next stop Tripoli. While she rounded out the picture by becoming the adored little thing he had left behind. While her snapshot would go with him in a watch. Required equipment. He had probably thought of it while getting measured for his uniforms and had called her up. Something to get starry-eyed over when far, far away. Also when awash with *vin rouge*. A candle glowing in the window. Leave it to Bill. The Sabine touch.

The trouble with Bill was that there wasn't anything the trouble with Bill. Even in looks the man hadn't missed a moth-eaten trick: slim flanks, broad shoulders from whose bulwarks he tapered via a washboard stomach to a lean waist, the current mode in faces which involved a patina of rugged virility to temper the too-handsome look, a voice like a deep and confidential bell. And boy, did he know it! He made her sick.

That was the phrase which had definitely terminated all conversation with the pilot. He heard her say after an hour's silence, and to his utter bewilderment: "He makes me sick." Then she had clammed up again, and he had spent the balance of the flight in wondering what he had done and in pondering upon the sad traces of congenital idiocy so prevalent in today's youth. It was with relief that he helped her down from the cabin and turned her over to a uniformed coachman.

The coachman said, "Your luggage will follow in the wagon, Miss Ledrick."

"Thank you."

The drive was magnificent over a graveled roadway with the full majesty of the Adirondacks rising around her, and the air carried an ex-hilaratingly clear odor of cedar and pine.

She said to the coachman's strapping back, "I thought that there were no roads."

He turned an urbane profile.

"There are none in the sense of going anywhere. Just roads like this one for connecting the house with the field and service places. We use planes for supplies or for any contact with the outside world."

"Even in winter?"

"Yes, Miss Ledrick."

"But isn't it like living on Mars?"

"My wife has occasionally pointed that out to me."

"I can imagine that she would."

"We have our amusements. There's a theater for the staff where the latest films are shown, an excellent library, a social hall, but—"

"But no new faces."

"Never, unless the steward makes a replacement or a change."

"Replacement?"

"Occasionally one of us dies in service. Most of us are of an age."

"Oh."

"Being here is like sailing on a ship for a voyage that has no destination."

"That's terribly well put."

"Thank you. I write for relaxation. A brochure or two on the feral in animals with its parallel among the criminal classes. Just ahead is our first view of Black Tor, Miss Ledrick."

Swift-deepening twilight made the house macabre with its turrets of stone and dark magnificence that presented, instead of a home, a bastion for defense. Ann thought of it as besieged and expected a moat, but there was none, and the victoria stopped on a flagged courtyard before an oaken entrance door which opened and released warm light.

A butler greeted Ann with courteous ceremony and said, "Good evening, Miss Ledrick. I'll show you to your rooms. The lift is over here."

Ann followed him across a marble parquet beneath the entrance hall's beamed ceiling and into an elevator, where he pressed a button for the third floor.

"I'm Washburn, Miss Ledrick. A phone call came through for you this afternoon from a Mr. Forrest in Washington. I explained that your plane would not arrive until now, and he said that he would call you again tonight at eleven."

"Thank you, Washburn."

The cage stopped, and Ann followed him along a hallway broken by mullioned windows into a charming living room done in Adam and with a coal fire lazily welcoming on the hearth.

"This door opens into the bedroom," Washburn said, "and beyond it are the dressing room and bath."

"Thank you."

"Cocktails are in an hour on the ground floor in the lounge. Just turn to your left as you leave the lift. Danning will take care of you. She will be here with your luggage. If there's anything you want in the meanwhile just use the house telephone. Miss Marlow regrets not welcoming you until seven, but this is her hour for feeding the ocelots."

Washburn smiled, bowed, and left.

So this, Ann thought, was wealth. Great wealth and the key to that kicked-around phrase known as gracious living. And who wouldn't want it and not be a dope? The thought of her clothes began to appall her. The mouse—that's what she'd be—in gingham alongside of a woman who had all this and ocelots. Even if she was here only on a job, full social contacts were involved, and Ann remained appalled. It was scarcely a milieu for the simply adequate.

She stood at a window and looked out into the deepening darkness within which firs and pines were sinking and where pressing peaks were flattening into profile against the night sky. She wondered what further outrages Bill had in mind for the telephone call at eleven.

He had probably forgotten to tell her that after he married her next Friday he would divorce her on Saturday. The man was certainly a ball of romance. Just an old-fashioned nosegay fragrant with the tender touch. No, not fragrant. Reeking.

Someone knocked, and Ann said, "Come in."

A man carried her bags directly into the bedroom and then left. A cheerful-looking middle-aged woman closed the door after he had gone and said, "I'm Danning, Miss Ledrick. I'll get your bath ready and then put out your things."

Ann thanked her and looked again at the scene below, drawn back to it by something that puzzled her. She realized that, more clearly in the thickening dusk, thin luminous circlets were growing visible about the tree trunks which lined such stretches of the roadway to the airfield which she could see.

"Danning, what is that?"

"What, miss?"

"Those phosphorescent circles on the trees?"

"They're bands of luminous paint, Miss Ledrick. We have to observe the black-outs even here, you know."

"But aren't they visible from the air?"

"No, the leaves and branches mask them."

Danning suddenly stood still in the bedroom doorway while her smile flattened, leaving her lips drawn. Then Ann noticed it too: a thin, high note prolonged into a tremolo suggestive of sharp agony. It sifted faintly through the hall door and struck Ann unpleasantly with an impact of shock.

She said, "The ocelots?"

"Oh no, Miss Ledrick. That's Mr. Marlow. The music room is just below us, and he always likes to play the organ when it takes him. He plays it very loud."

"When what takes him?"

"Pain."

CHAPTER III

Ann inspected herself in panel mirrors as the elevator carried her down. The full-skirted bengaline rag with its leaf-splashed blouse looked pretty good. Monkey trick, if you wish, but in no sense tin cup.

Marlow's organ playing had stopped, and even before it had stopped the initial soul-in-agony effect had calmed down into a fretful Bach. She hoped the week would not be overlaid with a querulous neuroticism. Danning had been fulsome. Mr. Marlow's "pain," she said, was not so much of the body as it was of memory, a dark memory which overshadowed his mind.

There were physiological aspects too: a heart condition, neuritis, and an anemia which during the past couple of months had become pernicious. Ann added all these up together and was confident that when she met Marlow she would come face to face with a palsied wraith.

The lounge, when Ann stood in its doorway, struck her as Hollywood size and splendidly done, in the sense that its furnishings were impressive but were happily lacking in any unlived-in or museum-like *rigor mortis*. The man who stood up from a chair near the fireplace and walked toward her carried an immediate sense of welcoming friendliness.

He was not nearly so gaunt as Ann had expected from Danning's catalogue of ailments. Certainly he was opaque. He bore his age well, and there was a simplicity and general kindliness about him which made Ann instantly forget that the hand which he offered controlled one of the great fortunes of the country.

"Good evening, Miss Ledrick. I am Justin Marlow. Come over and meet my cousin Estelle." He went on as he led Ann toward the hearth: "You'll find that her bombazine exterior really shelters the soul of a *femme fatale*. For the past ten or fifteen years Estelle has been posing as the mystery woman of Paris, but nobody would take her seriously. People put up with her solely because of her chef, who was a *cordon bleu* and who had the distinction of committing suicide, as we've heard, when the black market ran short of mushrooms."

A woman rose from a sofa and smiled agreeably and said, "Miss Ledrick, Justin is a complete liar. My role in Paris was that of a Cassandra. I told the benighted fossils exactly what they were heading for. They preferred to consider me mad and would have locked me up a hundred times if they hadn't thought me so filthily rich. The instant that gendarme look would come into their eyes I'd just put on another emerald. Do you like sidecars?"

"Very much, Miss Marlow."

"So sensible. I'm as American as they come, but this national fetish for dry martinis convinces me that the country is still in the thrall of barbarianism."

Ann sat on the sofa beside Estelle Marlow and tried to readjust the portrait she had formed of the woman with its reality. The exterior was not the bombazine one which Justin Marlow had advertised, but the effect was close: a variety of velvet purples over plumpness and a serene apple of a face under a cap of softly graying hair most simply arranged. The hands were dimpled and beautifully shaped. As a girl, Ann thought, she must have been a beauty of the milk-and-honey type.

Washburn served cocktails and canapés while a drugging amiability in the general conversation began to make Ann feel hypnotically at home. She caught herself considering that she had known these two pleasant people always and that this room was one with which she had been familiar not for a brief moment but for many years.

This sensation was so strong that Ann thought: There's something funny about this. Isn't it a little overdone? I'm a photographer brought up here to do some ocelots and yet all this warmth, this instantaneous acceptance into intimacy. Ann felt it genuine enough, but there it was. Perhaps they both were parched for a stranger. That could be. Living as they did. But if she could be flown in, why couldn't friends be? Why isolation, with the obvious effect of turning her presence into an oasis?

It was during Ann's second cocktail when Washburn came in and said to Marlow: "The field has just telephoned that Mr. Ludwig Appleby has landed in a chartered plane, sir. Shall I give instructions that he be driven to the house?"

It became simpler later for Ann to dissect the reaction which Washburn's statement caused. At the moment her impression was of a thunderbolt in miniature cracking the serenity of a clear sky, in miniature because both Justin and Estelle Marlow instantly recovered their poise.

But there *had* been that moment during which Marlow's emaciated and sensitive face had frozen into an expression of intense hatred, while Estelle Marlow's kind eyes had contracted and her lips had thinned, fashioning the homely apple look of her features into something close to virulence.

The moment flashed and was gone, and Marlow said quietly, "Yes, Washburn, do. Mr. Appleby will join us at dinner, and if we can persuade him to stay over please place him in the rooms next to mine."

"Very good, sir."

Washburn left, and the conversation resumed its casual course; that is, so far as Estelle was concerned. Justin said little, and though outwardly calm and attentively agreeable Ann saw that his thin, veined hands were gripping rather than resting on the arms of his chair.

Estelle, who was on France, continued placidly listing the destruction of her continental possessions. The chateau at Noilly which she had leased to a European embassy had been deserted by the ambassador, and of course when the Germans had occupied it its treasures were either stolen or destroyed. Fortunately her flat in Paris had failed to bemuse them, and as for money, they had let her keep one half of such sums as she had received through Justin's influence from the States.

"As for my jewels," Estelle said complacently, "I was rather clever about them. You see, my dear, they put me down as a harmless eccentric whom it paid them to pamper while they used me as a mint. They're terribly practical, you know. Have you ever met one?"

"Not while in action, Miss Marlow. Possibly some of our local brood."

"Oh, those. Well, they thought my ocelots just another lunatic foible and were completely indifferent to my taking them with me when I left. I had had special collars made for them with large studs, the tops of which unscrewed and under which I put the genuine stones from my jewelry. I had very good paste ones replaced in the settings. I permitted General von Heinmann to steal the imitations, and he was very happy about it all, and so was I."

"So the ocelots brought the jewels home?"

"Yes. You have no idea, Miss Ledrick, how frequently it pays to be considered odd. That is, if you have the bank balance to back you up. Otherwise they put you in an institution."

Ann listened and was conscious of the undercurrent of unease. She felt this undercurrent increasing through the passing minutes and more especially so with Marlow, whose knuckles were white when Washburn announced from the doorway: "Mr. Ludwig Appleby."

Ann saw Appleby unclearly at first as he stood at the room's distant end. He approached them slowly and became a tall, middle-aged man of heavy build with a shock of ink-black hair and bold features of the stamp, Ann felt, which practiced matrons would consider both informative and alluring. The lips, on closer view, were lushly thick.

Marlow had stood up. He did not offer his hand. He said, "Good evening, Ludwig. This pleasure is becoming increasingly frequent."

Appleby's voice was rich with assurance and with glutted good living.

"You're looking a bit better tonight, Justin," he said. "Not a day over your age." Then he turned his eyes thoughtfully on Estelle. "And you too, Estelle. Somewhat plumper, perhaps? I ought to chase you around the block."

Estelle said calmly, "After dinner if you wish, Ludwig. This is Miss Ledrick—Mr. Appleby."

Ann said, "How do you do?" and found that Appleby said nothing whatever.

He stood looking down at her with his prominent dark eyes during a pause that ended in a puzzled frown. He said, "This is most extraordinary."

Estelle said sharply, "Miss Ledrick has come up from Fanny Mistral's to photograph the ocelots."

"Oh?" Ludwig said.

Then he smiled.

CHAPTER IV

The dinner was in keeping with Fanny Mistral's forecast, and Ann was hungry. She did a good job on clear green turtle soup with sherry, followed by pompano served with broiled mushrooms, and cucumbers, all helped to their destination by a glass of Rauentaler.

The extensive charm of the dining room had stopped impressing her. A four-part Sheraton table had been reduced to conversational size, and (her appetite clipped of its edge) she was beginning to feel annoyed at the persistency with which Appleby, who faced her, was regarding her. She decided it was a speculative rather than a predatory look. It was irritatingly unpleasant.

Appleby said, while a saddle of mutton was being served, "Are you from New England, Miss Ledrick?"

"No, Mr. Appleby. Long Island."

"Really? I would have said New England. Boston, perhaps. Do you know Boston?"

"Most sketchily. Almost from a football point of view."

Appleby's voice tightened, and the interest in his dark, vital eyes sharpened noticeably.

"Do you," he asked, "know the Charings?"

It occurred to Ann that Justin and Estelle Marlow were suddenly not only silent but motionless as well. They had the waxwork look of effigies who were gripped in the drama of some situation which involved them strongly and which they were helpless to control. Marlow grew pale, and his anemic fingers were nervelessly quiescent on the stem of a glass which Washburn had just filled with champagne.

"No," Ann said, "I do not."

Ann heard Estelle Marlow sigh gently in the stillness with a breath that had been held and was, with relief, expelled.

Then Estelle took over with determination.

"Ludwig, there is no more reason why Miss Ledrick should know the Charings than that you should know the Osterbrooks of Paris. The Osterbrooks, Miss Ledrick, were a fanatic family from Indiana who enjoyed spending quantities of money in collecting worthless paintings that were so modern they had turned sour."

"I fail to see any connection, Estelle," Ludwig said. "After all, the Charings are Back Bay."

"There is no connection. I simply wish to change the subject. We will discuss the Secretary of Labor, Miss Perkins. That woman—"

Miss Perkins was taken apart through a heavenly thing which Estelle Marlow informed Ann was a gooseberry charlotte. Its mechanics, Estelle said, consisted in lining a charlotte mold either with slices of *génoise* or sponge cake, then dumping in gooseberry cream and chilling until firm.

The dinner (and Miss Perkins) ended. They returned to the lounge for coffee and cognac, after which two rubbers of bridge were managed in a heavy atmosphere which seemed to Ann to have been stripped of all zest. The pleasant intimacy which had been set up before Appleby's arrival was gone, and in its place was one which seemed to her as impending; just of what, she did not know.

All of their rooms were on the third floor, and Ann thought it kind when Estelle went with her into her living room and said that if Ann did not mind she would sit there for a moment and smoke a cigarette.

The coals were still glowing on the hearth and the room was so silent that the sound of an ember dropping was distinctly audible.

Estelle said, "Do you mind if I call you Ann?"

"Not at all, Miss Marlow. I'd like it."

"And I should be pleased if you would call me Estelle."

"Certainly."

"May I ask whether you have been happy?"

"Here? Now? Most happy."

"No, dear. I mean the years before. You're twenty-two, aren't you?"

"Yes, just. How could you tell so accurately? I mean, we're all supposed to look either younger or older."

"I asked during my telephone conversation with Fanny Mistral. I wanted to know the general sort of woman to expect, as you would be with us for a week or longer. Tell me, have your years been happy ones?"

"Very happy. Naturally there has been some lonesomeness since Father died last spring. There were only the two of us. Mother died quite a while ago."

"Then there is no one? Now?"

"There is a pleasant idiot in Washington named Bill Forrest who has made up his mind to marry me next Friday."

Whether it was a trick of the firelight or not, Ann could not tell, but Estelle seemed to withdraw in suddenly upon herself.

"And you, Ann?"

"I?"

"Do you intend to let Mr. Forrest marry you, as you put it?"

"I put it that way because the first news I had about it was when Bill announced his intention by telephone from Washington this afternoon."

"Mr. Forrest sounds somewhat bewitching."

"He is much too bewitching. He's so utterly sure of himself. He wants to take me off to the wars with him in a watch."

"A watch?"

"Bill has just joined the Marines, may heaven help them. Naturally he has to have a snapshot of a wife bravely smiling and keeping the home fires stoked. His mind works that way. It seems he has selected me. So far, Bill's nearest approach to a romantic gesture has been to call me up at four in the morning to relieve his insomnia. He is definitely not of the doublets-and-knee-bending school."

"Then it is nothing really serious?"

"I don't know. Honestly I don't."

"You said—Friday?"

"Yes."

Estelle sat for a while looking thoughtfully down into the glowing coals. Then she said, "Things happen so rapidly now in this world of ours. Nations have been conquered overnight while an empire falls in a matter of weeks." She threw her cigarette into the grate and stood up. She said, "Good night, my dear. Between now and Friday are five days."

"I'm certain I can do a good job on the ocelots before then."

Estelle dragged herself back from some thought that was obsessing her. Her eyes were faintly bewildered.

"The ocelots?"

"The pictures I'm here to do of them."

A flush started slowly at the base of Estelle's throat and then rose until it colored the soft milk tones of her cheeks.

"So stupid of me," she said quietly. "The pictures. Of course."

CHAPTER V

Estelle left behind her an unpleasant note which cooled the room and sifted it with doubts. It was odd, Ann thought, about the pictures. Estelle had unquestionably forgotten them entirely, which placed them in the category of being a device to get her up to Black Tor rather than a reason in themselves. The original charms of arrival were flitting, with the warm friendly welcomes and the swift induction into the status of a cherished old friend. In their place came a sense of oppression, an intangible smothering to snuff out a happy flame.

The telephone rang.

Bill said, when Ann answered it, "Ann?"

"Hello, Bill."

"How are you?"

"I'm fine."

"Are you sure?"

"Perfectly, Bill. Why?"

"I don't like your being up there. I've wrung it out of Fanny that you knew nothing about the Marlows. The man is a dangerous nut."

"*No*, Bill. I like him. He's friendly and he's kind."

"So was that agreeable gent who gave his wives the bathtubs. The better to drown them in. His neighbors adored him."

"Bill, you're crazy."

"I'm not crazy, but Marlow is. He's been off his nut ever since his son knifed his wife twenty years ago. I don't mean Marlow's wife. She was dead. The son killed his own wife and was electrocuted for it."

"Bill!"

"Marlow believed in his son's innocence. He and nobody else. It knocked him for a loop and he's still spinning. This pretty domestic tragedy took place right where you are, my dear. Have you seen the music room? "

"No. It's just beneath me."

"The scene of the crime. She was playing Chopin on a spinet. The ivory keys ran red."

"*Bill!*"

"A factual detail brought out during the trial. There were roads there at the time and gaiety and a happy, carefree social life. Marlow removed the roads after the electrocution and planted them with trees. I want you to know these things because I want you to snap the damned ocelots tomorrow and pack up and beat it."

"It still doesn't make sense. About Marlow's mania, I mean. Why wouldn't he want to shut himself up from the world? I tell you he's kind, Bill. Old, and sick, and kind."

"Let me shake your sweet faith with a couple of rumors about the joint. It's a charnel house."

"It's nothing of the sort."

"The Dame has it otherwise. Not only did Marlow believe in his son's innocence, but he is still trying to prove it. The son's wife was a Charing from Boston. It explains her fatal delight in spinets. The Charings are the sort who wear blinders against the present and use the past like vampires to nourish their blue anemia. This Alice Charing who got knifed had a corner on the family's supply of good looks. She knocked men flat. There was nothing wrong about her. She was tops in every way, but unless she had gone about in a thick crepe veil she couldn't prevent the lads from getting sunstroke. That's what they claimed."

"Who?"

"The prosecuting attorney. The motive for the crime. Fred Marlow went berserk in a jealous rage. The whole thing was foul, Ann. Alice was going to have a child, and they did a Caesarean and saved it. The mother was already dead."

"That's terrible, Bill. Terrible."

"I know it is. It's why Marlow went cuckoo. He fought like a tiger to clear his son right up to the execution. Then, off and on, things happened."

"What things?"

"This isolation business and a couple of gents who died."

"Murdered?"

"That's what they whispered over the teacups. One was a boyhood flame of Alice's, a Jerry Abbott. He's the one the state claimed drove Fred Marlow into the deed. Abbott was staying at Black Tor at the time of the murder. Abbott came back to Black Tor as a guest of Marlow several months after Fred Marlow was electrocuted. Abbott left Black Tor in a coffin."

"Bill!"

"Well may you exclaim. A hunting accident, my dear. Abbott tripped and blew the top of his head off. But I can promise you that tongues wagged."

"How about the other gent?"

"That was more subtle. A Machiavellian touch. A Boston man by the name of Frank Lawrence. A basket of fruits and *pâtés* was delivered at his bachelor nest by a messenger boy on Christmas. He lived alone and ate alone, and a jar of *foie gras* did the trick. They said ptomaine, and he was cremated in jig time in accordance with his known wish. Later, when Lawrence was ashes and the remains of the *foie gras* sunk wherever it is that Boston dumps its garbage, it was recalled that Lawrence had also been a flame of Alice Marlow's, as well as having been present at Black Tor on the day of her demise."

"It was all coincidence, Bill. Just gossip."

"Be that as it may. Black Tor abruptly stopped being considered an Adirondack health spot, especially in the opinion of the late Alice's former circle of gentlemen friends. It got a Name."

"I gather that."

"The Abbott-Lawrence deaths bred later rumors, all unpleasant and, I must admit, unconfirmed—they've a peach of a lake there where two people were drowned—and the ultimate conclusion remains that Marlow is as crazy as they come."

"You ought to get a spot on NBC for bedtime stories."

"This is no bedtime story. You pack up in the morning, Ann, and get out of there."

"I'm beginning to think that I will. It was all right until Appleby came. More than all right. It was delightful."

"Appleby? Appleby!"

"Yes, Ludwig Appleby."

"He's one of them."

"One of what?"

"One of Alice's old crowd."

"He asked me whether I came from Boston. He asked me whether I knew the Charings."

"Ann—you get out tonight."

"I *can't*!"

"No, I suppose you can't. And anyhow it would be Appleby's neck that was in danger, not yours."

"Honestly, Bill! You're such a comfort."

"Well, beat it in the morning. Ocelots or no ocelots. Just forget about it now, dear, and get a good night's sleep."

CHAPTER VI

Thunder aggravated the nervous and irritable edge of a night that had been divided between fitful sleep and hours of wakefulness in a house where murder and tragedy still left their bitter stamp.

Ann's watch said half-past eight, but the windows were sullen oblongs of dark lead ripped at intervals by a blinding jag of lightning, with a resultant shatter of the roar. And so, she thought, it storms. A typical mountain storm graciously sporting about the encircling peaks. In fact, right in her lap.

She rang for Danning. Her awakening moments were never of the witless type, and Ann grasped at once the assurance that all planes would be grounded at Black Tor until this local performance ceased. A torrential rain was accompanying the general bravura and slashed the windowpanes with frustrated bullets of water. There could be no tactfully swift departure until it stopped, all of it, including its effectively startling noise.

Trapped.

Momentarily the thought amused her, and her smile still lingered when Danning came in.

"Good morning," Danning said, and added, "What a day!"

"We could probably tell better if we could see it."

"It's because of the northern lights the night before last. They were all trailing and green, like loose fingers. They always mean one of these things within forty-eight hours."

"How long does one of these things last?"

"Two days, three days, then the sun comes out again. We usually get a couple of them during a summer. What will you have for breakfast?"

"Orange juice, coffee, and toast, please."

"That will never last you, Miss Ledrick. Have some creamed finnan haddock."

"I will have some with pleasure. It's difficult to break loose from the drugstore routine."

"I'm sorry there are no papers this morning. We bring them in by plane from Albany, but of course everything is grounded." A resounding thunderclap perioded the observation. "You can see what I mean."

"Indeed I can. Are these storms always so clinging? Don't they ever move over and pick out another peak?"

"Oh yes, they just circle around. Just about when you think they've gone for good they come back."

Danning left, and Ann saw no sense in waiting to have breakfast either *en negligé* or in bed. There were too many sound effects and far too much gloom for any svelte dawdling. She bathed and dressed and, going into the living room, found a birch log fire brightly burning and breakfast being arranged by Danning on a coffee table before it.

"Miss Marlow suggests that you join her when you've finished," Danning said. "Her rooms are at the end of the hallway. She thinks that if you brought your camera you might catch some interesting views of the ocelots because of the storm. She says it makes them atavistic."

"I can imagine it would. A good thunderbolt, and away goes that house-pet look."

"They're dears, really, and just as cute as they can be."

"How big are they?"

"Oh, about three feet long."

"Merely good-sized kittens."

Danning smiled and said they were like kittens in their own fashion, of course. Then she left, and Ann ate while briskly dissecting a resume of Bill's telephoned catalogue of horrors. What it amounted to in the cold light (black) of day was that Marlow's son Fred had been convicted of killing his wife and had been electrocuted.

All the rest was surmise and rumor. The shotgun could have gone off accidentally when Abbott tripped, and Lawrence's Christmas basket of goodies could conceivably have contained a *pâté* jar riddled with ptomaine. As for the two drownings in the pretty local lake, such gemlike bodies of mountain water were famous for their icy coldness and their general tricks. A plunge, a gasp, a cramp, a tombstone. Dreiser, Ann thought, in a sentence.

She collected her camera, some flash bulbs, and some packs of 2 ¼ X 3 ¼ super-fast panchromatic film, the emulsion on which was so sensitive that she felt assured of stopping all and any atavistic snarls in the fraction of a flick.

It occurred to her as she walked along the long hallway that all of Bill's horrors were not resolved. Appleby remained. Was he slated for lilies via the accident route too? Ann recalled Marlow's odd greeting of Appleby last night before dinner: "Good evening, Ludwig. This pleasure is becoming increasingly frequent."

Certainly barbs had lain in it. Of the most well-bred sort. An iron foot in a velvet shoe. But it hadn't bothered Appleby, and it inferred that his visits had been both numerous and on the impromptu side. And Appleby still hadn't broken his neck. Ann found it comforting.

She sensed a certain abstraction in Estelle Marlow's good morning, an abstraction which Estelle immediately explained by saying: "Justin has just gone through one of his distressing nights. I suppose that the storm may have accented it. I sat with him for a while after Dr. Johnson left. You'll forgive me if I seem somewhat blunted."

"Of course. I'm terribly sorry about Mr. Marlow."

"It isn't unusual, although his attacks have been growing more frequent. It's a wretched combination of neuritis and a pernicious anemia. Dr. Johnson is splendid. He stays here and has his own house on the grounds. He has brought in several of the best specialists for consultation, but I'm afraid—" Estelle's voice trailed off, then her smile came quickly, as though to reassure herself against dark thought. "Everything is being done. It's one of those lingering things."

"He seemed so well last night."

"He was well. But, as I say, the storm, and there are times when Ludwig Appleby upsets him."

Estelle did not pursue this. Instead she led Ann through a living room and into a duplex arrangement that had been converted for the ocelots' indoor use. A great skylight and an air-conditioning system made the place a conservatory suitable for the more modest of the Paraguayan trees up which the ocelots could climb and sit.

The cats were nervous and on edge. One was of tawny yellow ground color, while the other two were of reddish gray, and all were handsomely marked with black spots, streaks, and blotches. The tawny one paced irritably beneath a tree upon a limb of which his companions pressed in sullen plaques.

"I'd better stay until they get used to you, dear," Estelle said. "Will it bother your work? I know how artists hate being observed."

"No, I wish that you would."

"That one slouching around on the floor is Herriot, dear, and the two in the trees are Clemençau and Madame de Staël."

Ann put a film pack in the Graflex and took a few experimental shots. The flash bulbs, due to the competition of intermittent lightning-and-thunder effects, failed to impress the ocelots at all. She finished the pack with some close-ups and was removing it to exchange it for an unexposed one when Washburn came in rapidly and went at once to Estelle.

Later, when talking it over with Sergeant Hurlstone of the state police, Ann recalled in detail the things that she did with the exposed film pack just removed from the camera. She was replacing the protective covering about it and putting it back in its cardboard container while

Washburn was saying to Estelle: "Mr. Marlow requests that you come at once, Miss Marlow."

The urgency in Washburn's voice was reflected by Estelle.

"He is worse?"

"Considerably, I'm afraid. He requests that you bring Miss Ledrick with you."

(The film pack was now in its carton and the flap closed. Ann still held it in her hand. The camera was on the floor.)

Estelle said swiftly and with an intensity that made her voice vibrant, "Ann dear, come with me at once."

She took Ann by the arm and all but impelled her toward the door. The exposed film pack, closed in its carton, was still in Ann's hand.

"Quickly, Ann dear. Every moment may count."

CHAPTER VII

Marlow's bedroom was completely ducal. The bed, a massive piece still handsomely sound since it had served its purpose for Napoleon during the Empire, was lost in the room's proportions, and Marlow was comparatively lost in the bed. A uniformed nurse built on stolidly efficient lines stood on guard as Ann, still impelled by Estelle, came to rest at the bedside.

Marlow's face was drawn and pale, but his eyes were open, and their expression held the same kindliness which had been in them during his greeting of Ann last night. Both hands were resting on the coverlet, and their fingers seemed almost transparent in their thinness.

Estelle said with hospital cheeriness, "Justin dear, you startled us. You look splendid. Where is Dr. Johnson?" Marlow's voice was quite clear but weak.

"He is coming." He smiled at Ann. "Crises are usually attended by a touch of the ludicrous, Miss Ledrick. In this instance, a bath. Dr. Johnson will arrive dripping."

"I wouldn't talk too much, Mr. Marlow," the nurse said.

"Forgive me—Miss Ledrick, Miss Ashton. Miss Ashton is the Florence Nightingale of our community. As for the talking, I must do so while I can. Estelle, will you sit with Miss Ashton in the living room, please? I have something to discuss with Miss Ledrick."

"I shouldn't leave you, Mr. Marlow."

"You shouldn't upset me, Miss Ashton. Go, please—or you won't be responsible for the consequences."

Miss Ashton turned professionally anxious eyes on Estelle.

"You know how it is when he's like this."

"I do," Estelle said. Her eyes locked with Marlow's. "Are you *certain* this is wise, Justin?"

"No, I am not. Unfortunately it is imperative."

"Then come, Miss Ashton."

A flash and a deep roll of thunder shattered against tall windows as Miss Ashton followed Estelle from the room.

"You are thinking," Marlow said to Ann as the roar died away, "that this is most extraordinary, Miss Ledrick. It is."

"Naturally, Mr. Marlow."

"I am weak and find words increasingly difficult. Sit here, will you? Sit close to me."

Thin and translucent fingers patted the coverlet of the bed, and a strong revulsion of nervous fright gripped Ann. It was compounded of Bill's utterly horrible digest over the telephone, of the storm, and, oddly enough, of a montage-like mental picture of Ludwig Appleby and the Charings of Boston.

The revulsion passed rapidly, and Ann felt in its wake a recurrent liking and sympathy for this sick and, yes, dying old gentleman whose smile was begging her to understand some problem which obviously was presenting difficulties of the strongest nature toward being explained.

She sat on the bed. The exposed film pack was still in her hand. Marlow noticed it and looked at it for a moment reflectively.

"You were at work, Miss Ledrick?"

"Yes. Just one set of exposures."

"You like this work?"

"Very much."

His hand reached out, whether toward hers or to the film pack Ann did not know, but her reaction at the touch of his fingers was involuntarily to draw her own hand away, leaving the pack on the bedcover. Marlow's fingers closed over the pack, and he lifted it and examined it.

"Are you satisfied that photography offers you a career, Miss Ledrick?"

"There is nothing else that does, Mr. Marlow."

Again the thunder pealed, and Ann wondered while reverberations rolled and died away toward what point Marlow was with such difficulty driving. She felt it to be more than the accepted eccentricities of the old and sick and rich, some purpose that involved her precisely.

She noted that Marlow almost fondled the film pack for a moment and then kept it pressed in his hand, and the hand resting quietly on his chest. The impression was clear that he regarded the pack not as an object in itself, but rather as something that belonged to her and that holding it brought him a sense of comfort and of pleasure.

He said in the dead silence that followed the clap, "There is no time. I must come directly to the point, Miss Ledrick. You were brought here to Black Tor for a purpose. One utterly divorced from your photography or the portraiture of Estelle's ocelots. They were the device I employed for getting you to come. No—do not be alarmed. What I have done has been because I believed it to be the best. For you. I did so only after nights of torture and of doubt and the fear that my physical condition might worsen suddenly to a dangerous point. You shall be my judge."

Marlow's voice broke queerly with the effect of an engine suddenly bereft of power. He said, "I had a son."

"Yes. I know, Mr. Marlow."

"You are familiar with my tragedy?"

"I know what I suppose people in general know." Marlow's fingers tightened convulsively about the film pack, and he pressed it more closely against his chest, as though to conquer some inner pain.

"Then you know nothing, Miss Ledrick." His voice was very weak. "Nothing that specifically concerns you. I—some water, if you please—this brief distress—"

Ann stood up swiftly. He was dying. His eyes had closed. His lips were betrayed into a gentle flutter. In panic she ran into the living room.

She said to the nurse, "Miss Ashton, go to him. I am afraid Mr. Marlow is dying."

Estelle started to follow Miss Ashton into the bedroom, but some compulsion caused her to stop beside Ann and look searchingly into Ann's eyes.

"Did Justin tell you, dear?"

"He started to tell me something, and then his voice died away."

"*Tell me—tell me what he said.*"

There had been time enough by now for Ann to appreciate exactly what it was that Marlow had said, in especial concerning the pictures of the ocelots having been a device to get her up to Black Tor. She felt the normal anger of anyone when placed in the position of a dupe. Her sympathy and liking for Marlow dissipated, and with it ebbed her similar regard for his cousin Estelle.

Oddly enough, the more this former tide receded, the more strongly flowed a need for Bill. To see him, to talk with him, to go back to the rut of a placid normality.

Bill's telephoned commentary with its theme of charnel houses and madness lost its flip detachment and grew personal to herself. Some basis to it must and did exist and she, through dupery, was being woven into its pattern along with the devastating Alice, two swains, two unfortunate bathers, and an electrocuted son. Ann did not want to be included at all. She wanted only to pack at once and go.

Estelle observed her intently while Ann thought this.

"Justin did say something, dear. He said something which has distressed you. I know. I can read it in your face."

"Yes, Miss Marlow, he did. He admitted that taking the ocelots was nothing more than a device to get me up here. Why?"

"Oh, *that*—"

Estelle paused as the hall door swung open and a stout, harassed-looking gray-haired man nodded curtly to them and hurried into the bedroom.

"That is Dr. Johnson," Estelle said. His arrival brought her an emotional letdown, and she sank into a chair. "It has been a strain. I know how selfish that sounds. I can't help it. My life has been a taut wire for months. It has been especially terrible because there is nothing anyone can do. Each day, each tomorrow could have been the end."

Estelle closed her eyes and pressed dimpled fingers against her temples.

"You still haven't answered my question, Miss Marlow."

"Please—that contraption over there is a cellaret. Just lift the lid, dear, and it all comes apart. I'd like some bourbon, straight."

Ann opened the cellaret and got the drink. She handed it to Estelle.

"I must insist on leaving here, Miss Marlow. I shall go as soon as it can be arranged."

Estelle drank the bourbon. Her eyes became velvet pansies clouded over with tears.

"Ann, it is hard for me to believe that that is all that Justin said."

"He did add that this trickery was all for my own good. Is he sane?"

"Perfectly. Justin is one of the sanest and most brokenhearted men on earth. As for why he wanted you up here, I haven't the right to tell you. Only he can do that."

Then Dr. Johnson was back with them and saying to Estelle, "Not yet. I remain astonished at his stamina. Miss Ledrick?"

"Yes, Doctor?"

"Mr. Marlow asked me to say that he would resume his talk with you later. I believe he will be strong enough to do so toward five this afternoon."

"I will have returned to New York by then, Doctor."

"Oh? I gathered that you were staying for a while. Well, I shall drop in later, Miss Marlow. Good-by, Miss Ledrick."

"Good-by, Doctor."

Dr. Johnson opened the door, and Ann saw, standing in the hallway, the heavy figure of Ludwig Appleby. Appleby waited until the doctor had passed and then came in.

He said to Estelle, "How is he?"

"Better, Ludwig. But you know."

"Yes, I know. And good morning, Miss Ledrick."

"Good morning, Mr. Appleby."

His prominent dark eyes were lively with speculation. "Washburn tells me that Justin sent for you to come to him as well as for Estelle."

"Yes."

"You know, I find that very interesting."

"I found it so too, Mr. Appleby. I am returning to New York this morning."

"Are you?" Appleby waited until a crash of thunder had subsided. Then he said, "How?"

"That's it, my dear," Estelle said equably. "Of course if you insist we'll arrange for a plane to take you at the earliest possible moment." Her eyes turned vaguely toward rain-sheeted windows. "These storms are tiresome things, Ann. They last so long."

CHAPTER VIII

There was nothing left to do but pack. Pack and wait until a zero ceiling lifted and would permit a plane to depart. The camera was still in the room with the ocelots, and Ann went and got it. The three cats were completely indifferent to her and remained absorbed in their pre-captivity dreams while the storm hurled down tons of water with endless monotony.

Ludwig met her in the hallway on her way back. He was standing before the elevator door, but Ann thought that the scene was arranged: a chance position on Ludwig's part which he could hold indefinitely until he caught her on the return to her room. He bulked darkly in the storm-light gloom, and she experienced a sheer overpowering effect of bone and flesh. His smile was senseless with artificiality.

"Do let me," he said.

He had (before a wit could help her) the camera and the flash-bulb case in his hand and was opening her living-room door and ushering her in with remarkable expedition. He came in too. He placed the camera and the flash bulbs on a table. He offered Ann a thin gold cigarette case half filled with fat-looking cigarettes.

"Will you?"

Automatically Ann took one and thought, while Ludwig lighted it: He's turning it all on. All of the manner that he must have found (especially among dowagers) so thoroughly successful during these later years which, although hesitating on the plumpish, were still imbued with a hung-over virile force.

"Thank you, Mr. Appleby. And now, if you will excuse me, I intend to pack."

Ludwig remained rootedly stolid.

"You remind me of an aunt of mine. Aunt Deborah."

"Yes?"

"Yes. If she were starting on a journey on a Tuesday her packing would be done the week before. Her bags, in consequence, were always in a state of flux."

"I assure you that mine won't be."

"Justin said something that disturbed you?"

"I scarcely think, Mr. Appleby—"

"No, you are quite right. It is no business of mine." Ludwig's eyes, Ann noticed, were no longer on her. Rather, they were darting about the room in what surely were purposeful glances: observing the walls, the furniture, even the rugs. Why? It reminded her of her favorite criminal literature in which, before whisking open the wall safe, the principal scamp would first case the joint.

"But," Ludwig was saying, "I am curious. I am fond of Justin. Very fond. His attitude toward you, a stranger, has frankly made me apprehensive. I hint, of course, at hallucinations. Tell me, did he strike you as quite normal?"

Marlow hadn't. Anything but. But Ann had no intention of following Ludwig's lead into an open discussion of the manias.

"Perfectly."

"I am delighted to hear you say it. Even though it does leave me still far up in the air as to why you are suddenly decamping with the ocelots as yet not immortalized. Aren't you going to ask me to sit down, Miss Ledrick?"

"No, Mr. Appleby, I am not. I am going to pack."

Ludwig must have finished with his casing, because his bold dark eyes were again exclusively about her.

"Very well," he said. He gave her his best false smile. "I must be slipping. Perhaps I need a new technique."

He left.

Ann did not at once start packing. She put through a call for Fanny Mistral instead. The lines were not affected by the storm and shortly, via Miss Dingley, Ann heard Fanny's voice.

"What on earth was that background crash, Miss Ledrick?"

"Thunder," Ann said. "And more thunder."

"Of course. Those mountain storms. Grieg did them so much better. Why are you calling? Don't tell me that the ocelots are cowering under beds."

"No, I'm leaving."

"Leaving?" Fanny screamed. "My dear child, you can't. They wanted you for at least a week, and I am charging them for your priceless services at a daily sum which brings the roses even to my withered cheek. Spoil a thousand shots if you have to in your search for absolute and costly perfection, but for the love of Henry Morgenthau, Jr., do drag it out."

"They never wanted any pictures in the first place, Miss Mistral."

"Are you serious about this?"

"Perfectly. Mr. Marlow told me so this morning. He's dying."

"Dying?" Fanny screamed.

"Yes. He has just admitted that the pictures were only a device to get me up here."

"But why? That sort of plot went out with bustles."

"Honestly, I don't know what to make of it, but I'm getting out. Bill called me up last night and painted in the background."

"Look here—nothing has happened, has it? Along the more lethal lines?"

"No, I just don't like it."

"No slithering screams?"

"Not a groan or a shriek, but there'll be a few if I have to spend another night here, and they'll be mine."

"You're perfectly right, Miss Ledrick. Marlow must have gone completely insane. By all means leave. Leave now."

"I can't until the weather clears."

"Of course, the planes. Well, I wouldn't worry. It isn't a pleasant situation, but it's absurd to think there could be anything dangerous. How is the cousin? Is she gibbering too?"

"No, she's very nice. So is Mr. Marlow. I'm simply worried over having been brought up here by a trick."

"Justifiably so. Is there anything I can do? Would it help if I were to talk with Estelle Marlow?"

"I don't see how it would. She is perfectly agreeable to my leaving as soon as possible."

"At least keep in touch with me. I'll leave word with Dingley where you can reach me all day. Incidentally, what's Marlow dying of, or don't you know?"

"Pernicious anemia seems to be the base of it."

"Seems—hmnn! Take care of yourself, Miss Ledrick."

"I will. I'll pack now and wait."

"I'm sorry about this. Really sorry."

"You didn't know. I'm glad I called you."

"I am too."

"Good-by."

"Good-by, and, for heaven's sake, escape by pack horse if they start airing out the dungeons."

For several hours Ann found herself left alone. With the packing done, there was nothing left for her to do but wander restlessly about the living room and let the storm get more strongly on her nerves.

There were books and magazines, but she found it difficult to concentrate enough for reading, and there was little pattern to her thoughts. Shortly before one o'clock there was a rap on the door.

"Come in!"

The young man was a stranger. He wore an acid-stained smock and carried several 8x10 prints in his hand.

He said, "Miss Ledrick, I am Harley Brown. I take care of the photography lab. Mr. Marlow sent over the film pack you took of the ocelots this morning and asked me to develop them. He sent word that he wanted a specially good job done, as he wanted to show you how greatly he appreciated your work. Well, I thought I was crazy, so I made enlargements and—Oh, take a look, will you? Tell me if you see what I see?"

Brown put the prints on a table. The ocelots were stunning, but spread across the surface of each exposure, almost ephemeral in its faintness, was the silvery skeleton of the bones of a hand.

"Do you get it, Miss Ledrick?"

"Yes—like silver bones—"

"That's what I thought. And it's on all of them. Might be part of a hand. Those two could be fingers."

"They are fingers."

And Marlow, Ann remembered, had held the film pack in his hand, had kept it pressed against his chest.

"Mr. Marlow did take the pack in his hand," she said, "but I don't see what that could have to do with it. It might be a defect in the whole batch of film, of course."

"I've never run into anything like it."

"Neither have I. It's uncanny."

"I felt that way. I got sort of a chill. What do you think we ought to do? I don't like to show them to the old gentleman. His heart isn't any too good, and in the state he's in today it might kill him. Seeing bones like that."

"How do you get hold of Dr. Johnson?"

"You just telephone him. Why?"

"I want him to see these. It sounds impossible, but I think those bones are of Mr. Marlow's hand. They're like an X-ray shot. He might know the reason."

Dr. Johnson, ten minutes later, was impressed.

"How long did Mr. Marlow hold the film pack in his hand, Miss Ledrick?"

"For at least several minutes while I was with him, Doctor. He was still holding it when I left the room."

"Yes, I recall now that he also held it while I was with him. I started to take it away, but he said he wanted it because it belonged to you. Queer ideas people get in his condition."

"When Washburn brought the pack to the lab," Brown said, "he told me that Mr. Marlow himself had given it to him, so he'd probably been holding it in his hand until then."

"What time was that?"

"About an hour ago, Doctor."

"He held it possibly for three hours, then. Is the film especially sensitive, Miss Ledrick?"

"Very, Doctor. It's about the fastest emulsion there is."

Dr. Johnson shrugged helplessly and looked sick. Slowly the color left his face and it became gray.

"I couldn't have known," he said. "No man could have. I am faced with this, Miss Ledrick. I have been treating Mr. Marlow for neuritis and pernicious anemia. The symptoms are exactly the same as those for radium poisoning, when some form of the substance has been ingested. I mean, by that, eaten. As Mr. Marlow must have done. There is nothing on earth that can or could have been done to save him. To all purposes he is dead." A look of childlike amazement came over his face. He said, "It's murder."

CHAPTER IX

Thunder rolled, jarring with repercussive tremors all objects in the room and filtrating through animate nerves already vibrant and on edge. Dr. Johnson slowly dropped the prints back on the table.

Ann watched him, drugged by being face to face with murder, with the thought being still unreal, so divorced was it from all of the things through the years of her life which she had known.

Harley Brown watched him, caught in a similar state of inanimation, while Dr. Johnson placed the prints side by side, face up. Dr. Johnson seemed to have not the slightest awareness whatever that he was doing so. His jowly face, which held suggestions of at some time, years ago, having been handsome, appeared stunned and frozen while his voice, when he spoke, held the measured cadence of groping thought rather than of speech.

"This thing must have been going on for months, possibly for a year, many years. There is no way of telling for how long. No earthly way of knowing when the radioactive substance was given to him. One ingestion would have been enough. It would never have to be repeated. One little speck, so small it could have been a sugar seed upon a cake."

Dr. Johnson looked at them helplessly, as if beseeching them to join in his wonder at this enormity for which he was so unprepared and against which all of his knowledge of science, which ranked among the highest in the country, offered him no weapons for combat.

"Are you going to tell Mr. Marlow?" Brown asked.

"I don't know. I do not know what to do. What we are faced with is a man who is murdered and yet who is not dead. There is this about life: I must prolong it. I must keep it fanned until it dies of itself. His heart is bad. To tell him of this would be for me to kill him, to snuff out that flame I have been nourishing with such trouble, with every resource that I know. You see that, don't you? Both of you see it?"

"Yes," Ann said. She threw away her irritation at dupery and thought again of Marlow as a kind old man. She was suffused once more with pity for him in view of this horrendous act which had been done against him, with its recognized fate for which there was no known reprieve. Such time as was left him with its peculiar burdens of physical and mental pain, why weight it down further and add the gall of murder to his already bitter cup? She said, "What does it matter?"

"You catch my point, Miss Ledrick. The thought of retribution. Possibly Mr. Marlow alone could let us know toward whom to look, could give us some definitive indication as to his murderer."

His murderer, Ann thought, is one of two people: his cousin Estelle, who presumably would inherit Marlow's great fortune, or Ludwig Appleby, whose motive would be enmeshed in the decades-old murder of Alice and the electrocution of the son.

Who else?

Dr. Johnson was regarding her curiously, and he said: "No, do not jump at the obvious, Miss Ledrick. I can sense that you are making people suspect and are delving for a motive. I suggest that both you and Mr. Brown disabuse your minds of restricting Black Tor as a haven for the murderer. The very nature of the crime makes the possibilities most broad."

"In what way?" Ann asked.

"Because we do not know and may never know just when the radioactive substance was given Mr. Marlow. Months ago, surely. Perhaps years. I am thinking of the dark days following the death of his son. You know about those things?"

"Yes, Doctor. The common reports."

"Then you know nothing, really. I lived through them. I think I may say without boasting that I made it possible for Mr. Marlow to live through them. Night and day it was a problem of keeping his mind from going to pieces. I shall never forget. And this deed could have been done even as far back as then. I remember many people came here, people whom Mr. Marlow wished to question and observe. There were members of Alice's family, her mother, Elizabeth, and her father, Morton Charing. Even though mourning had started to be an anachronism, Elizabeth Charing seemed shrouded in black, a white dot of a face lost in crepe. That was all before Mr. Marlow's great seclusion. Before we became this shut little world."

Dr. Johnson thought for a while and then said: "There is the law. Man's law and the one of my profession. I hope a compromise can be arranged. I will telephone the state police and make a report. I will tell them exactly how things are. So much we must do." The decision seemed to please him, for he shook off his lethargy and said: "Mr. Brown, have you spoken of these prints to anyone other than Miss Ledrick or to me?"

"No, I brought them straight up here."

"Was anyone helping you in the laboratory?"

"No, Doctor."

"I would not care for people to know about them. It would not be wise. In spite of what I have just said to you, Miss Ledrick, we cannot blind ourselves to any possibility. If the one responsible for this evil business *should* be among us and should learn that his plot has been discovered—well, even that confuses me. Because what further mischief could he do, beyond speeding with some swifter means Mr. Marlow's already certain end?"

"What will I do if Mr. Marlow asks to see the prints?" Brown said.

"Couldn't you say that the films did not turn out?"

"He wouldn't believe me. He knows the Mistral people's reputation."

"Blame me," Ann said. "Say that I saw them and wasn't satisfied. Say I destroyed them during a fit of my alleged artistic temperament."

"Good," Dr. Johnson said. "Will you take care of them, Mr. Brown?"

"I will, Doctor. And the films."

Brown picked up the prints and went toward the door, and Dr. Johnson followed, saying: "This is not pleasant for you, Miss Ledrick. It cannot be helped."

"I know that, Doctor."

They left her, and Ann sat down and smoked a cigarette. It failed to soothe her, and her nerves grew increasingly jumpy. The sullen weight of storm light had not abated, and the room's lamps tempered but did not dispel the general gloom.

She considered calling up Fanny Mistral again and then thought not. To tell Fanny would be to tell the world, and tomorrow's papers, if the storm permitted them to come through, would reek murder and revel in a celebrated corpse which still was living and had breath.

Estelle or Ludwig Appleby would then read the report and would not let Marlow speak. One or the other of them would see to that. Dear Justin (this was Estelle), let me cool your fevered brow. And dimpled fingers would press, slipping tenderly downward over cheekbones to the windpipe. Hello, Justin (this was Ludwig), feeling better? Then a solicitous approach to the bedside and, with hairy, thick-set fingers, the same result. Ann felt sick.

There was a knock, and Estelle came in and Ann felt sicker.

Estelle's face was still rosy and applelike, and all of her soft plumpness radiated its aura of kind good will toward all men. So strong was this aura that Ann repudiated Estelle from the villains' corner and settled on Ludwig Appleby. Surely Estelle must be rich enough not to want more money, with her chateaux and Paris flat and emeralds now so cannily home with her, thanks to the ocelots.

Whereas Ludwig presented a murderer cut in the grand style. The man was cast to type.

"Ann dear," Estelle said, tentatively reaching out dimpled fingers and then withdrawing them, "do come down with me to lunch. I feel so stupid about this business of your having been brought up here for another reason than your photography. Really, dear, it's not a modernized version of *East Lynne*. Justin will be able to see you this afternoon, and then you will understand perfectly. Accept the situation for a little while, no matter how melodramatically outrageous it may seem to you." Estelle glanced toward the windows. "In any case, you'll have to. And we're having squabs crapaudine and babas with kirsch for dessert. Have you ever had squab that way?"

"No; in fact, rarely any way."

"I wish you could see Henri fix them. He cuts the breasts and turns the two ends so as to look like a frog and then flattens the result with a blow of the cleaver. It makes him very happy, and I have to send down a little note of appreciation."

She did not know. Estelle could not, Ann thought, know and still be pleasured with such warmly gustatory anticipations. Ann was swamped with sympathy for this agreeable woman who was trying so hard to be friendly and over whose head, impregnant in the very atmosphere which surrounded her, hung death in its most brutal form.

They went down to lunch.

Ludwig Appleby put himself out to be pleasant. He indulged in no thoughtful glances or in any of the complex innuendoes with which he had bespattered Ann last night and during the morning. Estelle seemed grateful for this change of Ludwig's, and the babas arrived during a swelter of chitchat of the most innocuously social nature.

Dr. Johnson came in while they were having coffee.

His face was pouted with worry, and his skin had the quality of damp suede. He apologized briefly for intruding. He refused Estelle's immediate invitation to join them.

He said to Ann, "Mr. Marlow wishes to see you. Will you come with me, please? Now?"

He said to Ann as they walked toward the elevator: "Mr. Marlow recovered consciousness and started talking about you. Inadvertently I mentioned your decision to leave here today. I would not have done so if I could possibly have foreseen the effect on him. He became frantic. He insisted upon my giving him something which would bring him momentary strength, enough strength so that he could talk with you."

CHAPTER X

The nurse and Dr. Johnson left, walking softly on the carpet's deep pile: two stolid rears, the one in dark tweed and the other planed in starched white.

Ann sat in a chair drawn close to the Empire bed, its metal stars golden in murky light, its smooth veneers deep pools of dark shadow.

Marlow's skin was waxen, and his eyes were abnormally alive from the stimulant which Dr. Johnson had given him. They searched for Ann's eyes, held them compellingly.

"My life has been like this storm," he said. "Thunder and lightning crashing close and then receding to a murmur. But never going, always coming back again. Do smoke if you want to."

Wasted fingers gestured toward a marquisette box on the bed table. Ann took a cigarette and lighted it.

"I know very little of your life, Mr. Marlow. I've been told the general rumors, that's all."

"Do you believe them?"

"No."

"Why not?"

"Because I've met you."

This pleased Marlow enormously, and he said nothing for a while but lay quietly regarding her, and then he said: "I had nothing to do with the deaths of Jerry Abbott and Frank Lawrence. I am reputed to have killed them both. You have heard about them?"

"Yes."

"Also, there was that business of the two men whom I managed to drown in Crystal Lake. So it was said, and so it still is said. Such rumors never die. They have the longevity of burdocks. I grew tired of people tightening up when they came near me."

"I'm sure the deaths were accidental, Mr. Marlow."

"You say that because you have decided to like me. As for myself, I am sure that they were not. They were murder. I except the two men who were drowned. But Abbott and Lawrence, a common thread united them, one which bound each of them to Alice, and I am incredulous at so great a stretching of coincidence. What do you know about Alice?"

"She was your son's wife."

"I shall say it for you: and Fred was executed on the charge of having murdered her. I shall tell you about Alice."

"I have been told she was beautiful."

"Very beautiful. Can you understand that her beauty was not just a thing of the day? So many handsome young women receive the cachet through a resemblance to some reigning fad. Because they looked like the Gibson girl or some timely belle of the hourglass age or the statuesque. We find their pictures in old albums and realize that their beauty died with their brief moment, leaving tolerant laughter. Alice was not like that. She had a timeless beauty, both of face and of character. It killed her. Much as the ownership of some celebrated jewel is potentially linked with violence and death."

"I would like to have known her."

"You would have loved her, as Fred loved her, and I. She was a simple woman, natural and sweet and utterly incapable of governing this devastating power which her beauty gave her. It constantly bewildered her, and I think there were moments when it frightened her too. I want you to understand this because I want you to understand Fred."

"I think I do. Covet is such a bad word, but I can see how she would be, as men would covet a stone like the Koh-I-Noor."

"Yes, that is it. Covet, kill, and cheat, and die as men have always done for such a thing. It has never been the stone's fault any more than the fault was Alice's. She was as inanimate in her helplessness as that. Mr. Richardson, who prosecuted for the state, claimed that Fred killed her during a fit of homicidal jealousy."

"I know."

"Clarence Harlan was our lawyer. He still is. I told him then, as I still tell him today, that Fred's sole chance of proving his innocence lay in our turning up the man who killed Alice. My intention to do this has never died." Marlow raised himself on one elbow while the scarlet silk of the spread rippled in dull valleys of fire. He forced himself to speak, in the manner of a man who has reached the brink of an abyss and is, at last, compelled to jump. "*Your* intention to do this must never die. There was a child. You are that child."

Shreds came back of her civilian-defense Red Cross work, and Ann thought: I'm getting shock. Clammy skin, feeble pulse, lassitude; all were evident because her admirably cultured power of intuition assured her that Marlow would never have made such a confounding claim unless it were the truth.

"I have shocked you," Marlow was saying, "but I am a believer in clean strokes rather than in a niggling approach. Clarence Harlan is one of the best lawyers in the country. He has all of the documentary evidence of this, Ann. You were not given over into adoption. So far as you and the world were to know, you were simply brought up by Florence and Walter Ledrick as their own child."

"I loved them, and they loved me. They were everything to me."

"If I had not been sure of that you would never have been left in their care. You are no longer a child but a woman. You now have the moral stamina to accept this situation which would have shattered you during your formative years, warped you, driven you deeply into some neurosis from which you never could have recovered. Instead of being the healthy girl you are now you would have been an embittered, furtive creature, wincing before every finger that pointed you out as the daughter of a murderer, of a husband who had killed his wife who was with child. Could you have stood that, Ann?"

"I think no child could have."

"There was also the brutal misfortune that you were heiress to a great fortune. You were news. You would have continued to be news at every break you might have attempted from any seclusion. School, social contacts, a normal girl's existence would have been plain hell for you."

Marlow waited until his breathing had calmed down and then continued: "You were three months old when I arranged with the Ledricks that they take you. They and Clarence Harlan guarded the secret. No one else has known it until recently I told Estelle. Naturally the press made great efforts to discover what had happened to the Marlow Murder Baby." Marlow smiled bitterly. "They gave up the search in time as a bad job."

"And now, of course…"

"Yes, you will go through your moments of anger and torture at their hands, but you will have the courage and strength to face them." Marlow leaned toward her and said with dreadful earnestness: "And you will have the courage to carry on my fight after I am gone. Your fight, Ann. You shall prove your father's innocence, never pausing, never letting up until the job is done. No—do not interrupt—I am growing weak."

Marlow fought for breath for a moment.

He said, "I have sent for Clarence Harlan. Everything that I know, he knows. Give me your hand, Ann."

Her own fingers were as chill as Marlow's. He pressed them gently.

He said, "You will need your courage. All of it. Not alone from the publicity you will be forced to face, but from physical dangers. When you leave this room it will be known that I have told you every guiding point I have been able to discover leading toward the murderer of your mother. There are not enough, but you and Harlan will add to them. Complete them. I have guarded myself well." (You have not, Ann thought. Your guard has failed. You have been murdered.) "I am going to arrange plans whereby you shall be guarded too. Trust no one. Trust no one but Clarence Harlan."

A spasm of such strength gripped Marlow that he twisted sideways across the bed. He fought desperately for breath, but the power to breathe eluded him, and his eyes grew weary of the strain. Briefly the struggle ceased. He died.

CHAPTER XI

Ann felt no sense of grief over Marlow's death because of the short moment for which she had known him. Certainly there was none of the wrenching sorrow which had shaken her after the deaths of Florence and Walter Ledrick, whom she continued in her heart to consider as her true mother and father.

She was sorry for Marlow, enormously, and thoroughly shocked. Her skin remained clammy and chill while she waited in Marlow's living room after Dr. Johnson and the nurse had gone in to him.

Dr. Johnson returned alone.

He said, "Mr. Marlow is dead, Miss Ledrick."

He observed her speculatively. He shook a pill from a vial in his pocket and got a glass of water. He made her take the pill.

He said, "A fearful experience for you. You are shaken, but your sense of shock will be over shortly. Mercifully his passing was quick, and at last we can come out in the open."

"About the radium, Doctor?"

"About everything. I shall get in touch again with the state police and let them know that death itself has solved our impasse. I see no reason for locking these rooms until they reach here. There is no 'scene of the crime.' Simply a bed in which a murdered old man died." He smiled oddly. "Of course it's more than that. There's an end-of-a-dynasty touch about it. He was a great figure in his way. One of the last of those men who were so rich that their lives touched the feudal. You are looking better, Miss Ledrick. Some color is returning to your cheeks. Miss Marlow must be told. Would you care to come with me?"

"Yes."

Dr. Johnson hesitated.

"Do you mind my being curious? I am puzzled by what he wanted to see you about. In a sense whatever he said to you would fall under the heading of being last words."

"He told me, Doctor, that I am Ann Marlow."

Dr. Johnson's once-handsome face became deathly pale, and small mottle marks grew prominent on his skin.

"I brought you into the world. I did that operation which made it possible for you to live." He studied Ann for a moment with eyes that were newly critical. "How wise he was. How right. Tell me—Alice and Fred Marlow are nothing more than names to you?"

"Nothing more, Doctor."

"So completely wise." He contemplated her for a further moment as a visual justification of Marlow's apt foresight. He seemed to regiment some disturbing train of thought. He said, "Does Estelle Marlow know this?"

"Mr. Marlow said he had told her."

"And Ludwig Appleby, does he know?"

"No, Doctor."

"I am being stupid. It doesn't matter now whether Ludwig knows or not. The country will read of it in tomorrow's newspapers. You will be the most talked-of woman in America."

They took the lift to the ground floor. An utterly irrelevant and untimely realization came to Ann as they were descending. She thought: This is my elevator.

It symbolized with deadly accuracy the fabulous change in her fortunes. Her work had taken her into many great houses, and more than anything else their private lifts had stood out as the hallmark of large wealth. She had been touched with a normal envy.

She felt badly about thinking of such things with Marlow so newly, so brutally dead, but the notion had come and had burst like a small star of white fire in her brain. She admitted the truth that subconsciously she would have liked unlimited wealth. That any woman would have. The Cinderella dream so deathless in each of them. Aladdin's lamp.

Her father (she would always, she thought, continue to regard Walter Ledrick as such) had once tried to shield her against future disillusionment when she was a child. He had said to her: "The gods, to avenge themselves, grant us our desires," and had explained what the quotation meant. It recurred to Ann now.

Estelle and Ludwig were playing backgammon near the fireplace in the lounge. The rattle of dice seemed impudently futile on the heels of a crash of thunder. Both of them, when they observed the look on Dr. Johnson's face, stood up.

"Justin," Estelle said, "is dead."

"Yes."

Tears brimmed her eyes.

"Justin. I think of him as sleeping. A good sleep at last with no horror in his dreams." She held out her dimpled hands to Ann. Ann took them.

A delicate scent of Parma violets sifted from Estelle. She said, "He told you, Ann?"

"Yes."

Ludwig's bold dark eyes were no longer alive with speculation but were flat disks of knowledge.

"You are Alice's child," he said. "I knew it last night when I met you. I thought of her at once on seeing you. I thought of her while talking with you this morning. You have her look."

"Who is with Justin, Doctor?" Estelle asked.

"Miss Ashton."

"I must go to him. Death is so unbelievable when it comes, no matter how much one has been prepared for it. This is hard on you, Ann. I'll carry on until you get adjusted. There are any number of people to be notified and things to be done."

"I have already," Dr. Johnson said flatly, "notified the state police. I phoned them before lunch. Before, even, Mr. Marlow's death."

Ann could see Estelle shrink. Literally Estelle seemed to get smaller, and her face looked as if someone had struck her. She regarded Dr. Johnson as though he had suddenly gone stark mad.

She said, "Why?"

"Mr. Marlow was murdered."

Ludwig gripped the edge of the backgammon table so abruptly that green and white counters rolled slamming onto the floor.

"How was it done?" he asked.

"I shall make my report to the police."

"I see. It's going to be that way."

"Ludwig!" Estelle said sharply. "Poor Justin. Even to the end." She sat down as tears once more clouded her eyes. She said to Dr. Johnson, "What do we do?"

"We wait." Thunder growled endlessly. "Possibly they will get through on horseback. I'll telephone now."

"Is there anything to be done here?"

"Nothing. The coroner must get through, too, before Mr. Marlow's body—before any arrangements can be made."

Dr. Johnson left the room. They sat with their several thoughts. A log shot sparks up the chimney. Death seeped down upon them, through wood and steel and plaster, from Marlow's room. It descended unchecked by any physical barrier and joined them.

"Ludwig, would you mind leaving me with Ann?" Estelle said.

Ludwig was not pleased. His handsome face clouded sullenly, and for a moment he seemed on the point of refusing.

"Very well," he said. "I'll be in the library if you want me.

Estelle waited until Ludwig had gone. Then she said to Ann, "Do you know the fable about the man who protested too much? It isn't a fable, of course. It's one of those things out of Shakespeare. Anyhow, it's Ludwig. He was here when Alice was killed. He has always claimed that he knew something which might prove Fred's innocence, something which lay just on the fringe of memory but which Ludwig was unable to recall. Justin has been giving him sums of money at different times for years to jog this peculiar quirk in Ludwig's memory. Ludwig is not a pleasant man."

"No, he is not a pleasant man."

"Of course Justin never believed in him for a minute and neither have I. Justin paid to tempt him into coming here. He hoped that at some moment during their talks Ludwig would make a slip." Estelle glanced briefly toward the distant doorway. "Justin and I have always thought it was Ludwig who murdered Alice."

CHAPTER XII

Washburn apologized for the interruption.

He spoke briefly of Marlow: a formal expression of sincere regret at his death, offered both to Estelle and to Ann. His manner toward her, Ann thought, had subtly altered. She was, it implied, now one of the family.

The press associations, Washburn said, and a great many specific newspapers were putting through telephone calls with requests for interviews and information. The story had been phoned to the New York *Review* by its local correspondent in the village of Bypass, from where the troopers were leaving on horseback. The *Review* was already on the street with it, and the other papers were insistent for further facts.

Washburn looked at a point impartially spaced between Estelle and Ann.

"What would you advise, Estelle?" Ann said.

Estelle reached over and gave Ann's hand a warm, friendly press.

"Let us leave them to Washburn, dear. Perhaps it would be best to say, Washburn, that a statement will be given out after the proper authorities reach here. It is always a wonder to me that that phrase doesn't drop apart from habitual senility every time it's used. I know you won't antagonize them, Washburn."

"No, Miss Marlow."

"For your sake, Ann. They'll make a Hollywood premiere of you as it is, without this ghastly horror of Justin's murder being tacked on. You had better say, Washburn, that Miss Ann Marlow will be very glad to give interviews when she recovers from the shock of her grandfather's death. She is at present resting under the care of Dr. Johnson. Is that all right, Ann?"

"Thank you, Estelle."

"There is a personal call," Washburn said to Ann. "Miss Fanny Mistral from New York. Will you take it, Miss Marlow?"

"Yes, of course."

Ann followed Washburn to a small room just off the lounge. He indicated the telephone. He closed the door.

"Darling!" Fanny's voice screamed. "The *Review* had it on the streets two minutes ago. I simply can't believe it. I feel as if I've been using the Hope diamond for a paperweight. Are you all right, darling?"

"Perfectly all right."

"My dear, you're a woman of iron!"

"I'm glad you called. It's like something solid, hearing you, or doesn't that make sense?"

"It's the most insulting thing that's ever been said to me, and I love it. That man who sent the story in from that unheard-of village in the Adirondacks told simply nothing. Just that you were that child and that Justin Marlow had been murdered. I shan't ask a thing because I know the AP and UP will commit murder themselves to get the story out of you, and I do appreciate the fact that you can't talk. Especially to me, darling. I know me. Clarence Harlan is the Marlow lawyer, isn't he? "

"Yes, Miss Mistral."

"For heaven's sakes," Fanny screamed, "call me Fanny! You're rich enough to now. Well, every word you say from now on will have to be infra-rayed by Harlan. My dear, you'll love him. I met him last fall at one of those dogfights that Mariot Whipple calls luncheon, and he's the nicest old lamb that ever housed a wolf and ate a grandmother. He'll probably dash in on horseback ahead of the troopers, and don't think he can't. Is there *anything* I can do?"

"Thank you, Fanny, nothing. But it has been ever so good just hearing you."

"You'll be staying up there, won't you? That's stupid. Of course you will. And *don't*, my dear, look demure when the troopers give you the third degree—just be candidly *soignée*, with a dash of the clinging-vine and the sloe-eyed touch. I know those breeched hot cakes. What?... Wait a minute, dear."

"I will."

"Darling, I couldn't be sorrier. Miss Stevens just dashed in and said that eight vultures from the press have wrecked the joint and gone off with every shot we have of you. They even took those grim things Davis did. You remember when he tried that new lighting and turned you into a reincarnation of Zaza? Oh, my *dear*!"

"It doesn't matter, Fanny."

"You'll find out whether it matters or not when you get the morning editions. Just sue me as much as you want to. Good-by, darling, and call me any minute of the day or night you feel you need a solid."

"Thank you, Fanny, and good-by."

Ann hung up. She returned to the lounge feeling extraordinarily better from her chat with Fanny which had given her, in effect, a momentary release into the outside world. Relief was stripped from her when she saw that Estelle had gone and that Ludwig, instead, was sitting on the sofa by the fire. Flat in her mind was Estelle's calm statement that Ludwig was a killer. The killer.

She said stupidly, "Estelle?"

"Estelle, my dear Ann, has gone up to Justin's private office to preside over a joint session of his estate manager and his secretary. The welter of details pursuant upon the death of a man of your grandfather's prominence is enormous. Sit down and have a drink with me. I've just sent for one. You look all right on the surface, but you must be completely ratty inside."

"I'm not."

"Well, you should be. After such jolts. Personally, I intend getting slowly and methodically cockeyed."

"I'm going up to unpack."

"I told you you reminded me of Aunt Deborah." Ludwig said with sudden intensity, "Look here, what was it?"

"What was what?"

"What killed Justin? Was it a knife? A gunshot? Was it poison? Weren't you there?"

"Yes."

"Well?"

"It was radium poisoning. He had eaten some radioactive substance."

Ludwig's expression of intense interest grew blank. He thought this over for a while. Ann thought the beefy redness of his cheeks was paling.

"That's rot," he said. "How could Johnson determine a thing like that?"

"The skeleton of his hand was developed on films I had taken of the ocelots. He had held the film pack in his hand. Dr. Johnson will undoubtedly explain it more technically to the troopers."

Ludwig said nothing to this. He sat shrouded in his thoughts which were, Ann decided, assuredly of the darkest sort. She left him and went toward the door.

Ludwig said as she reached it, "You're very clever, Ann. Aren't you?"

CHAPTER XIII

Ann went on up to her rooms. She was fretful, nervous, and completely at sea. Nothing had sunk in. She was still Ann Ledrick with a job at Fanny Mistral's and a room on Thirty-sixth Street.

She didn't feel rich. Not even partially rich, much less Marlow rich. This very detachment from her changed status tempered greatly any sense of nervousness about immediate physical dangers. There was no assurance of reality to punch it home.

It was curiously difficult to accept Ludwig in the killer role just on Estelle's say-so. Even his recent bravura of ignorance as to the method of Marlow's slaying—although it could have been a spurt of calculated histrionics, it could also have been perfectly genuine. Estelle was herself too apt a subject for the part to take her word alone.

Ann removed her things from the luggage and put them away. She visualized with a certain irritation Ludwig's Aunt Deborah as she did so. While this normal activity lasted it shoved Marlow's tragic moment of death and his burning warnings into a general remoteness and dulled their edge from reality.

But he had been murdered.

There was always that. Murdered for having circled ever nearer and nearer to the murderer of Alice. Murdered, of course, by the murderer of Alice. And Marlow had handed her the torch. Whether Ann wanted it or not did not matter. She held it.

She could protest herself blue in the face that Marlow had died before having told her of the spadework already done. His (and Alice's) murderer would never believe it for a minute and, in any case, would realize that Clarence Harlan, when he reached Black Tor, would shortly give her all the facts.

Her ears, attuned to the intermittent rumblings of thunder, failed to catch the knocking on the door until it was repeated. She opened the door and saw the silhouette of a stranger, dark against the sullen light which dulled the hall through its mullioned windows.

"I am Martin Thurlow," the man said. "I am the estate manager."

"Come in, Mr. Thurlow."

"Thank you."

Thurlow stepped in. In the living room's stronger light he offered, with his neat, rimless glasses and thinning sandy-toned hair, a portrait of efficient precision. His movements were all accurately timed and nice, and his smile was as thinly clear-cut as the pressure of the hand which he offered to Ann.

"I came to offer you both my sympathies and my services, Miss Marlow."

Ann thanked him and suggested that he sit down. She was relieved at having him here, at having anyone on hand to interrupt the dark and irritated turgid mess of her thoughts. Thurlow struck her as refreshingly impersonal and solid, very much like the human adding machine which he probably was.

Then thunder ripped tumbling through the sky, and she wondered, while its peals prolonged and then muted off, about Thurlow.

Why shouldn't an estate manager fit in among a suspect list? The manager of a property the value of Black Tor easily could. The accounts which passed through Thurlow's hands must be enormous and could present opportunities for peculations which, no matter how modest in themselves, could sum up to a handsome total through the years.

She revolted at this state of mind she was settling into: one of constant suspicion. Thurlow was probably as honest as the day was long. And boy, she pondered in passing, was it long! He looked so certainly an agreeable, businesslike, clever man.

"Miss Marlow suggested that I drop in," Thurlow said after the last disgruntled rumble of the thunder. "She asked me to say that she herself will come as soon as the most pressing things are gone over with Fleury. There are innumerable wires to send and cables."

"I thought that Mr. Marlow had cut himself off from people?"

"He had, but his former friends must be notified just the same, and his business holdings reach rather largely throughout the world. Most of them, fortunately, lie in South America."

"What was his business, Mr. Thurlow?"

Thurlow smiled slightly.

"Everything, I suppose one might say, and none. Your grandfather had an uncanny sense for making both timely and sustaining investments. He exemplified extremely well the man who did not put all of his eggs in one basket. During recent years he entrusted quite a few of his interests to me. They were in addition to my regular job of managing Black Tor."

Thurlow had been looking with more than usual interest around the room.

"I wonder whether you know that these were your mother's rooms?" he asked.

"No, I didn't."

"It's the first time they have been used since her death. It was one of Mr. Marlow's foibles to have them kept locked. I must confess I found it rather interesting when I learned they were to be opened up and put at the disposal of an artist in photography. A stranger." He stood up and smiled pleasantly. "There was a good deal of speculation about it among the staff, I can tell you."

"I can see where there would be."

"Yes, it is understandable. We have had so very little to speculate about during these years of our exile from—yes, I might almost say from life."

He said good day and went to the door, where he paused for a moment to take a more comprehensive and more leisurely look at the pleasant room.

"A charming setting," he said, "for the charming woman I understand your mother to have been. How extremely wise Mr. Marlow was to have shielded you from her tragedy. If he had not, you would today be a replica of what he was himself, the shadow of a living person, wasted, embittered, and shrunken from daily brooding on that terrible event. You know, I doubt whether you could ever have brought yourself to stay in these rooms. Yes, I think you might even have been afraid to. Well, good day again, Miss Marlow."

He closed the door.

CHAPTER XIV

That, Ann decided, was a good swift jab with anybody's needle. Just what had Thurlow meant to imply by his curtain line? For it was one, and handled in the very best manner of the Clyde Fitch school. All he had needed, she thought irritably, had been a mustache to twist.

Was it a warning, or was it a threat? She shrugged. You pay your nickel. Best let it go at that. She did look the room over with fresh eyes. So it had been her mother's, her true mother's: that figure of tragedy who awakened no emotion whatever in her beyond a stranger's pity.

The dreary monotony of the storm and this standing around and waiting with nothing to do had nourished her nervous irritation to a fine point by the time Estelle came in shortly after three. Fleury was with her.

Fleury didn't, Ann thought, help much. He fitted in perfectly with the general gloom. With his gauntness and with eyes that were of shallow blue and were shutters rather than windows to his thoughts. His left arm was wasted and distorted.

"I want you to know Mr. Fleury, dear," Estelle said. "Justin depended on him so much. You and I must depend on him now for so many matters concerning Justin's affairs of which we are ignorant."

The shutters lifted for a moment as Fleury accepted Ann's hand. It effaced the expiring-fish effect and gave her a glimpse of the real man. There was force. A lot of it. There was an undercoat of force even in the reserve with which he greeted her. She knew he was sizing her up, obliquely now, and not regarding her potentialities as a person but rather as an instrument upon which, at some later moment, he purposed to play a tune.

Fleury did not linger. Having paid his respects, he left them, and Estelle said, "You noticed his arm, of course?"

"Yes."

"Justin did it. Justin always did drive like the devil when he was younger. It wasn't from recklessness but simply from a conviction that when he bought a car which was built to go a certain speed with safety he saw no reason for not using that speed when he felt like it. To him it was just an understandable business proposition. Well, he hit Fleury."

"But how terrible!"

"Yes, it was. It wasn't really Justin's fault. He was doing one of his wild-West approaches along the driveway when Fleury stepped out into the road from the shrubbery."

"Couldn't he have heard the car?"

"Yes, but he wouldn't. Fleury is usually so up in the clouds that he rarely hears anything."

"Then how on earth is he a secretary?"

"He wasn't a good one. He was a very bad one, but a dear friend of Justin's had asked him to take Fleury on. Justin hated to fire people, but he had just about made up his mind to fire Fleury when the accident happened."

"I suppose then he felt obliged to keep him."

"Yes. It wasn't only the arm at the time. Fleury was pretty badly knocked about. It will be hard for you to realize it after this glimpse of him, but he was quite handsome, in that burning, ascetic way which was so fashionable right then. He adored Alice. From afar. We were completely cruel about this adoration and used to make it the subject of little jokes which were in extremely bad taste. We weren't an especially nice generation at the time, dear. And I doubt whether we've improved."

"I don't see why Fleury stayed."

"Well, people do. Justin loaded him with hospitalization and specialists and money and made his job more or less of a sinecure. You'll find as you grow older, Ann, that even idealists are not unswayed by good sound cash. They'll keep right on beating their breasts, but they'll accept the gold whenever their hands have a free moment. Fleury is an idealist, of course. Almost a rabid one. And I'm a thoroughly beastly cynic. I look for clay feet before I even glance at an idol's head."

"What are Fleury's isms?"

"All of them. Socialism, mostly. I'm interested in seeing how Justin's legacy will affect him. Justin left him a hundred thousand outright. My bet is that Fleury throws his share-and-sharings straight through the window and becomes an out-and-out capitalist." Estelle lighted a cigarette. "Ann," she said suddenly, "there must be a great many things you want to know."

There were, and foremost among them was some clarification from Estelle about Ludwig being the murderer. She would have started on this, but Estelle said, "Aren't you honestly curious?"

Then Estelle observed her for a moment and said, "No, I really believe you're not."

"About what, Estelle?"

"The estate. Surely it must mean something to you suddenly to know that you are one of the world's richest young women?"

"This will sound extremely stupid, but I don't realize it."

"Then let me bring it home to you."

Estelle plunged into a listing of Justin's far-flung holdings, the scope of the sources from which he had derived his great fortune. She went farther. She spread out before Ann the endless fields for pleasure and for acquisition which her huge income would give her.

Jewels, costumes, great estates, yachts, all of the things which (Ann caught this clearly) Estelle herself held of value in life, a glittering rapacity which, from her own standards, Estelle was transferring to Ann with the assurance that they would be equally acceptable.

"It is odd," Estelle said after she had finished with the dazzling parade, "what rotten tricks comparisons can accomplish. I'm not a poor woman. Far from it. But in contrast with what your income will be, I'm little short of knocking at the poorhouse."

"Surely we will share everything, Estelle?"

"No. I know Justin's will. He spoke to me quite frankly about it. He has left me a trust fund. A very good one, incidentally. He was afraid of this very streak of generosity you are showing now. He also knew as well as I do that I'm a greedy woman, insatiably so. My attacks of insomnia are all brought on by frustration over thinking up new things to buy."

"You shall buy whatever you like."

"My dear, to come right down to earth, the trust fund is broken if I accept anything from you at all. Justin knew me far too well. Of course if you were to die before I did and were an old maid, that would be another matter, and both contingencies are as improbable as the chances that this storm will ever stop."

"It does have an eternal touch."

"No, Ann. You must believe me. I am perfectly satisfied with what dear Justin has left me. More than satisfied. Grateful. It will enable me, after this terrible war is over and France rises again, to return there."

"Estelle, I've never understood that."

"*Expatriés*? I've not, myself, been able to satisfactorily. We're a queer breed. An atavistic throwback to our Old World roots doesn't explain it. What I really suppose it is just common sense."

"How can it be? Leaving your country?"

"You're young, Ann. I felt a twinge of that, too, at your age. Even recently, while last in Paris, there were moments of nostalgia. Some idiot ordering ham and eggs or a pancake. But there are many single and useless rich people like myself. We're deadwood, really, in any social scheme. What difference does it make whether we clutter America or Europe? We do neither any good. It would be different if I were married and had children. I'd stay here then."

"But why don't you like it better here anyhow?"

"I've tried to, dear, but I prefer the Continent. I'm aging and getting mellow, and the tempo of the Mediterranean coast suits me better than Palm Beach. For one thing, they have a greater understanding of single middle-aged women than we have over here, and, for another, the servants fight better, and that keeps my wits sharp. You are different. You belong here."

"I think I'd hate to live anywhere else."

"I'm sure you would. You and—his name is Bill, isn't it? Bill Forrest?"

"Yes."

"Has he called you since the newspapers started their fanfare?"

"No, he hasn't."

Estelle smiled serenely and started for the door.

"I must rest awhile. God knows what the troopers will be like. I need an hour's sleep or I'll greet them with all the social graces of a first-class zany."

Then she said before closing the door, "Don't worry about Mr. Forrest's not calling. He will. My dear, I envy you the happiness you have in store."

Do you? Ann wondered. Do you, Estelle?

CHAPTER XV

Sergeant Hurlstone of the state police reached Black Tor shortly after four o'clock. With him were Clarence Harlan and Medical Examiner Bedmann. The electrical pyrotechnics of the storm had stopped by then, but the rain continued to torrent down in gray cascades and the three men, in spite of their ponchos, were soaked.

At a quarter of five the house phone in Ann's living room rang. Ann answered it.

"Ann Marlow?" a strange voice said. "I'm Clarence Harlan. I'm coming in to see you, if I may."

"Certainly, Mr. Harlan."

"I've bailed myself out, but I'm still waterlogged, so don't expect anything more than a sodden old hulk. How about asking Washburn to send up my usual depth charge of rum, will you? I need it."

"Of course I will."

"Thank you. My rooms are just a quarter of a mile down the hall. I'll be right over."

Ann phoned Washburn and asked for the rum and also a scotch for herself. The backlash of Estelle's little visit had put on the bite, and Harlan's voice had come as a relief.

There was a good deal of mulling to do over the things which Estelle had said, Ann realized after Estelle had gone. Principally that salon handling of their mutual life expectancy with its connotations in Marlow's will: "Of course if you were to die before I did and were an old maid, that would be another matter, and both contingencies are as improbable as the chances that this storm will ever stop."

Well, the lightning had stopped and the thunder.

Harlan knocked and came in.

Ann liked him instantly. She doubted whether she had ever seen a man so completely ugly or with such a warming smile. He was not especially tall or large, and yet he lumbered. Comfortably. His clothes were so much expensive sacking. They were also (which Ann did not know) so much expensive tailoring by one of the best men in New York to give him precisely that wholesome look.

No male juror had ever sat watching him without feeling pleasantly satisfied with his own little blue serge number, and no woman juror had ever failed to want to give his coat a motherly twitch. Harlan had also discovered that this worked out admirably in private life, so he had never bothered to be svelte.

He shook hands and said he was going to call her Ann. "And you," he said, "will call me Clarence. I don't mind the name a bit. It saved me the bother of looking for chips when I was a kid. Where's the rum?"

"It hasn't come yet."

"Rotten service. Ought to change your hotel. I won't offer sympathies to you about Justin, because I know he could have meant so little to you. Just the death of a stranger. Same way when we get to that business about Alice and Fred. Your whole mentality and heart are still Ledrick, and that's how it should be. Both of them were fine."

"You knew them?"

"Intimately, only you never knew it. Part of the arrangement. Even to wish me a good morning is supposed to cost the wisher a mint. Stupid, the way a legend will grow up about a public figure. You'll find out. You're one yourself now. Has Bill called you up since the story broke?"

"Bill? You know Bill Forrest?"

"Ann, there isn't a thing about you that I haven't known since you were three months old. You lived as the Ledricks' daughter, but you were still the Marlow heiress and, thank God, here's the rum."

Ann answered the knock and said, "Come in." Washburn ushered in a manservant with a tray on which, among innumerable other things, was a spirit lamp heating a silver pot of boiling water. The man placed the tray on the coffee table by the fireplace and left. Ann thanked Washburn, who told her that Miss Estelle Marlow had suggested they would have cocktails in the lounge at seven. Miss Marlow had felt that the usual household routine should be adhered to if this was agreeable. Ann assured him that it was, and he went out.

Harlan mixed Ann a highball and then concocted, elaborately, his own hot spiced rum.

"Bill hasn't telephoned at all today," Ann said. "Fanny Mistral has."

"I like Fanny. I admire her. She's like a smart trick. You know it's legerdemain, but it's of the slickest sort. I guess Bill's busy being a marine. He is not, incidentally, a bad bet."

"For me?"

"Certainly. If you love him. And if you can get him."

"Get him! He's a direct descendant of Og, the caveman."

"True, but he is also a descendant of a sterling line of self-sufficient Forrests. Most of them had the major characteristics of Army mules. And the scene has changed. Bill isn't clubbing simple Miss Ledrick on the head. He's clubbing the Marlow heiress on the head."

"As if that would make the slightest difference to Bill."

"Possibly it won't. It's all according to how you handle him. You will be seeing Sergeant Hurlstone shortly, Ann. He's all right. He has brains, brawn, and believes in the decencies. A good character. I have given him a complete synopsis of your life, including the how and why of your being here now. Don't worry about him. Just help him. And now tell me everything you know about Justin's death."

Harlan sat quietly, sipping the hot rum as Ann did so. He made no comments. He did not interrupt. He seemed to weigh and separate and file her words as she spoke. She ended with the short talk which she had had with Estelle after Marlow's death and with Estelle's calm statement that both she and Marlow thought that Ludwig Appleby had himself killed Alice.

Harlan, at this, permitted himself a grunt.

"If Justin did think that he never said so to me. And why didn't he accuse Ludwig directly during his talk with you? From what you've told me, Justin's remarks were entirely general and vague. Either the close-ness of death was clouding his mind or Estelle was lying."

"Why?"

"I don't know why. But the fact remains that we have always consid-ered Ludwig the one person with a perfect alibi. Ludwig's clothes were wet."

CHAPTER XVI

Harlan mixed another hot rum. He suggested a highball, which Ann refused. He returned to his chair and for a while regarded the dark and rain-drenched windows.

He said, "There is the falsest sort of security in being cozy. As we are now. A lazy fire, soft lights, good drinks, and the intimate charm of this friendly room. Ships are like that, right up to the moment of some swift and unpredictable disaster. I am frightening you?"

"Not really."

"I think a little, I want to. Justin was right, Ann. Hold a constant alert against the unexpected in danger. Let me show you the murderer's mind. The murderer of Alice and Justin. To him you are an unknown quantity. He has no yardstick as yet with which to gauge you."

"In what way?"

"Your tenacity. The extent and strength of your purpose to carry on where Justin left off. I am interested in the results of Bedmann's autopsy. He is a good man, a careful one. I expect that the murderer's long-range plan involving the radioactive substance lingered too long."

"You think a swifter, an immediate poison was used too?"

"We shall see. There is nothing in all you have told me to indicate that Justin had come upon some decisive clue, but the murderer could have harbored that illusion. He will continue to harbor it and will believe that Justin passed the clue on to you. I shall get you out of here."

"I wish you would. I ride. You made it on horseback; why couldn't I?"

"We found the difficulties almost insurmountable even in daylight. We are centered here in a circumference of chasms, peaks, and streams. The streams were already swollen to torrents. There is no chance by night. We will see what weather the morning brings. I am hoping that the storm will be sufficiently spent for a plane to take off. You will be safer in New York. I will tell you about Ludwig."

"His wet clothes?"

"Yes. It was a day like this one. Buckets of water since morning, and about the same time of year as now. You have met Justin and Estelle.

You know Ludwig, Dr. Johnson, and me. We were all here. Have you met Fleury?"

"Yes, just an hour or so ago."

"He was here too. He had been Justin's secretary for just about a year. Hermits are outmoded, I believe. We dub them misanthropes or solitaries. Anyhow, Fleury turned into one after the accident. You know about that, of course?"

"Estelle told me."

"Well, when he got back on the job Fleury would scuttle out of his own apartment on the floor above only when Justin had some business for him to take care of. As you saw, he is permanently crippled. You can understand how sensitive he is about it."

"Of course I do."

"It is depressing to look at him, poor devil, and Fleury knows it. Anyhow, he's the one who found Fred in the music room. Fred had the knife in his hand and Alice was dead. Jerry Abbott and Frank Lawrence, naturally, you don't know."

"They were the hunting accident and ptomaine?"

"I agree with Justin that they were not accidents. Both were here, and that completes the list. You must think of all of us at that time as being twenty years younger, with emotions that were far more fiery and with far less balance than today. Estelle was twenty-five, very rosy-cheeked and plump, very much like any Christmas calendar version of a country lass, only give her a thumping income. And the only corn-fed thing about her was her figure. She was death on chocolate creams. Dr. Johnson, of course, was a far better-looking man at thirty than he is today."

"Wasn't that rather young? For him to have been Mr. Marlow's physician?"

"He was Alice's doctor, not Justin's. His father had been the Charing family doctor in Boston. The old gentleman had died of a stroke, and Dick had taken over his practice. Dick Johnson had graduated with about every honor in the book and was the boy marvel of Back Bay. To return to Ludwig. You can see what a bull he is."

"Indeed one can."

"Twenty years ago he was a younger one. Still very bull and he-man to the word go. Everybody else stayed indoors that afternoon because of the storm. But not Ludwig. Oh no. Ludwig had to pop outside and breast it. Just himself and the rain and the thunder."

"I bet he batted the bolts right back."

"No doubt of it. Well, he did look up at the music-room windows just around the moment when it was settled that Alice was stabbed. That's when he saw it."

"Saw what?"

"The thing that Justin paid him money for years to remember. It was a white back."

"A what?"

"Either somebody in a shirt, or a white coat, or a white dress. Rain blurred the window to an extent, but Ludwig insisted there was something identifiable about the white back if he could only put his finger on it. He is still claiming it and he still hasn't put his finger on it."

"Didn't he testify at the trial?"

"Yes, but it got us no place. We showed that Fred had been wearing a dark suit when Alice was killed and how improbable it was for him to have taken off his coat in order to stab her, especially while blinded in his alleged moment of homicidal rage. We insisted Fred's story was true: that he had come into the music room and found Alice stabbed and had taken the knife from the wound. We offered the white back as that of the murderer. The prosecuting attorney simply sliced Ludwig's frail impression into ribbons."

"Do you believe Ludwig? Estelle told me that she and Mr. Marlow didn't."

"I believe nothing, but I am again puzzled at Estelle because I've always felt that Justin did put some credence in Ludwig's story. Naturally we looked into this business of the white back thoroughly. Both Alice and Estelle were in dark dresses, which takes care of the women. The men were in tweeds, so there you are. And there was Ludwig with his lucrative claim. He grew more definite bit by bit as the years passed. It wasn't a shirt or a coat or a dress. There was something, he said, unique about it. I think it will remain unique as long as he can get a cent out of it."

"How *could* he charge for trying to help?"

"Oh, my dear Ann. Nothing so crass as that for Ludwig. He would ask for loans to tide him over momentary straits. Every time he got a loan from Justin he would then oblige by going into his famous concentration act."

"Estelle was definite about Mr. Marlow paying Ludwig simply because he hoped that Ludwig would make some incriminating slip and give himself away."

"Estelle would seem to have become peculiarly definite of late. But quite possibly she is right. She herself may have turned Justin to that point of view since her return from Paris. I haven't been up here at Black Tor in over a year. But I maintain that Ludwig's alibi was perfect."

"Doesn't that in itself—?"

"No, I know the current mode, and it's nonsense. The man with the perfect alibi is always It. I stick to simplicities, especially so in the case of Alice. There was nothing premeditated about the crime whatever. A flash of terrific passion, a weapon at hand, and she was dead. Have you been in the music room?"

"No."

"It has a museum flavor. Cases of rare coins, some excellent folios, some weapons. That was true to form, if you wish."

"The weapon?"

"Yes, a Cellini dagger out of one of the cases. Now Ludwig's alibi was this: Fleury raised perfect hell the moment he spotted Fred holding the dagger and Alice slumped on the spinet keyboard. I mean really hell. You wouldn't think Fleur had it in him. The lung power. Well, Ludwig had just come into the house by the front door. He was drenched clear through and left a clear trail of wet footprints right to the coatroom."

"Did anyone see him come in?"

"Not actually, but Washburn ran into the entrance hall because of Fleury howling murder, and he saw Ludwig just taking off his sodden overcoat."

"It was a matter of water."

"You are thinking of shower baths, of some form of trickery. Forget it, Ann. Nothing was planned about Alice's killing."

"This is something I didn't tell you. When Ludwig came here last night Mr. Marlow didn't act like a man who was glad because someone whom he was trying to trap had arrived. He looked murderous. You know how you can't mistake certain facial expressions? Mr. Marlow's was one of hate. Bitter, intense hate."

Harlan thought this over.

"Interesting," he said. "And odd about Estelle's several contradictions. She's such a clear-thinking woman usually."

CHAPTER XVII

Danning, the maid, came in shortly after Harlan had gone. A pale Danning and a thoughtful one.

She said, "I'm glad it's you. We always felt the child would come back one day. We knew that before Mr. Marlow died he would send for her, and I'm glad it's you who are Ann Marlow."

"Have you been here since that time?"

"I was one of the upstairs maids. I used to take care of Mrs. Marlow when her own maid was on vacation. Do you know that these rooms were Mrs. Marlow's? "

"Yes, Mr. Thurlow told me so."

Danning continued to chat at intervals while she drew a bath and laid out Ann's dark voile dinner dress. It began to occur to Ann as she watched her that there was a touch of the trancelike in her movements. Several of them would have been quite *de rigueur* at a séance.

"Mrs. Marlow was lovely," Danning said. "She was a poet as well as a fine musician. Often I'd see her sitting at that desk over there, writing, and she'd look up at me and smile. But she wasn't seeing me. I suppose you will think this is funny, but there are times when I can feel her in this room."

Danning lingered on this, tasting it mystically and standing back a bit with her head tilted to one side to consider its full effect.

"No," Ann said, "that isn't funny. Anyone you've liked—when you're in a place that is intimately associated with them."

"It's more than just that. I'm a seventh daughter."

This stumped Ann. All she could say was: "*Are* you!" It satisfied Danning perfectly, and she went on a bit about her extrasensory prowess.

"I saw my niece once."

"Saw her?"

"Yes. It was about four o'clock in the morning, and she came through the closed door and stood by my bed."

"You *did* say closed?"

"Closed and the bolt shot. My niece was at Newburgh at the time, hundreds of miles away. I knew she wasn't dead, but I did know very strongly that she was in danger from some grave illness. She was. The crisis had just passed."

"You heard from her?"

"I got a wire the following day from my sister Mabel. Influenza." Danning artistically savored Ann's reactions. "I hope I'm not making you nervous?"

"Not a bit."

"Some folks don't care about staying in rooms that have vibrations. I always say it's according to the vibrations. Your mother was so lovely and so kind, I'm happy when she vibrates. Has anyone shown you that portrait of her?"

"No. Where is it?"

"It's in the next room, the one your father used to use as a study. Would you care to see it?"

"I'd like to very much."

Ann went with Danning into the adjoining room, and Danning switched on lights. The portrait hung above a mantel.

"Mr. Marlow sometimes thought of having it brought down to the lounge, but he never did. He left it here because it's where your father used to enjoy looking at it."

It was a stunning job, and Ann saw at once that there was a resemblance. Quite a pronounced one, really, and she understood fully Ludwig's puzzled look on meeting her last night.

Danning sighed happily.

"I can feel her. Yes, I can feel her right now."

Danning, on this note of triumph, left.

Well, Ann thought as she returned to her living room, there is something to it. You do feel things. Not always with a seventh-daughter virtuosity, but still in a manner highly snorted at by scientists. She tried to shake off this train of thought before it became a mood.

Definitely it was not a moment for moods which impinged on the astral. Tangible murder was wretched enough. And where *was* Bill's brash voice? As Estelle had so kindly inferred, the Washington papers would surely be carrying the story by now.

Joining the Marines did not involve a retreat into solitary confinement. Anything but. They were famous for their aptitude with telephones. And telephone numbers. Well?

The mood took root while Ann did a final job on her lips and hair. As she sat before the dressing table it occurred to her that Alice had sat there too. Seeing the portrait of her mother had brought her nearer to reality, but still Ann, in all honesty, could not emotionalize her as such.

She went through the living room, and her eyes rested briefly on the desk where Alice had sat with her verses and loveliness and inward thoughts. How easy, Ann thought, to *think* a ghost. And how insultingly nonessential all mediumistic paraphernalia of floating cheesecloths and iced rubber hands.

This nervous reflection went with her along the hallway and into the lift, which once more impressed her with its cachet of luxury as Ann went down. It was somewhat before seven, and the lounge was empty except for the brawny figure of Sergeant Hurlstone toasting his rear before the log fire.

Ann found him everything that Ludwig Appleby hoped himself to be and wasn't. Features of calm granite, muscles of flexible granite, and eyes of hard dark slate. Practically a park monument of the better and more martial sort. He came forward to greet her, extending a hand which pressed her fingers with the courtesy of a restrained stone crusher.

"I regret the incident of your grandfather's death, Miss Marlow. You are Miss Marlow?"

"I am, Sergeant Hurlstone."

"I like to have things confirmed."

"A very sound idea, I should say, in your profession."

"It is. Mr. Harlan has told me about you. After dinner I would like you to tell me yourself."

"I'll be glad to."

"I will also want you to tell me every word you can remember which has been said to you since you arrived here. As well as everything which you have observed."

"I will do the best I can."

"That will be satisfactory. There is no such thing as perfection. Thank you."

That scene was over. Sergeant Hurlstone withdrew into his granite fastness and once more offered his rear to the co-operating fire. Ann sat on a sofa. Socially the moment presented no routine avenues for advance, and she regretted not having Estelle's salon touch: an ability to breach all walls.

She wanted to ask about the autopsy results or progress and saw no reason why she shouldn't. She was about to, when Estelle's entrance checked her. Estelle was loosely hung with nervous dark chiffons, which were relieved about the throat by a magnificent circlet of what surely were the ocelot-transported emeralds.

Martin Thurlow and Fleury were with Estelle. She introduced them to Sergeant Hurlstone while Washburn supervised the service of canapés and cocktails.

Then Clarence Harlan came in with Ludwig, who gave indications, it seemed to Ann, of having made at least one leg along his course toward becoming potted. Medical Examiner Bedmann did not show up, nor did Dr. Johnson.

Ann found herself with Fleury. He wasted no time but dived abruptly into his favorite ism.

"I suppose all this will go," he said.

"Black Tor?"

"Yes. The time has gone by when such gestures are any longer tenable. When lands and houses and machinery, when the lifetimes and ingenuity and labor of many women and men should all be expended toward the maintenance of privacy for a single individual. I do not think you will find the thought revolutionary. What will you do with all this, Miss Marlow? With these possessions both living and inanimate which now are yours?"

"I have still to appreciate that they are mine, Mr. Fleury."

"You are offended. You feel it an impertinence on my part. Do not. I have discussed this quite openly with your grandfather. I did not find him sympathetic."

"Sympathetic to what, Mr. Fleury? "

"To my notions, if you care to call them that. He did." Fleury's shallow and pale blue eyes took on some warmth of life. The shutters raised and revealed a glow. His notions were, he told Ann, frankly socialistic. There was nothing new about them. The administration in Washington for a good many years had been attempting to apply them, but such an attempt was due to be a long struggle and an ultimate possible failure.

You couldn't do it that way: from the top down. Using either a schoolmarm's admonitory finger or a big mouth or a big stick, to say nothing of making people pay through the nose for the experiment whether they liked it or not. No. That bred outright antagonism or a cumulative irritation, which was worse. You had to start at the bottom with a willing guinea pig who would offer himself as a proving ground; say a man like Mr. Marlow and with an outfit like Black Tor.

Fleury clearly was becoming feverish about his obsession (it amounted to one) when Ludwig joined them. He put his empty cocktail glass on a tray being offered by a manservant and took a filled one.

"Something tells me," he said to Ann, "that Fleury is off again. His face has that transcendental glow." Then he said directly to Fleury, "You might at least wait until Justin is decently buried before slicing up this elegant estate for a general handout. Seriously, what would you do with it, anyway, if some miracle were to put it in your hands? Do you seriously suppose that your selected little group of underprivileged souls would become so many contented bees, each busy on his own small patch? The harmonious lot of them sweetly stuck together with nectar and honey? You know it's rubbish. They'd fly at each other's throats within a week. You'd have a first-class massacre the moment Mrs. Puddlewick's neighbor stuck a new feather in her hat."

Fleury said with strange dignity, "We cannot hope to have Philistines understand us, Mr. Appleby," and walked away.

"Poor wretch," Ludwig said. "In my heart I'm sorry for him."

"You have a unique way of showing it."

"That's because I'm a little tight. I told you, Ann, I would be. But I was right about Fleury, wasn't I?"

"Yes, in a sense."

"For years I used to warn Justin to get rid of him. Pension him off or wrap a fortune around his neck, but anyhow get him out of the house. I don't like fanatics. I think they're dangerous. They're all of them borderline cases. Just the thin breadth of a hair between what shred of sanity they possess and in going completely overboard."

"I do think it queer that Mr. Marlow didn't in some way arrange to have him go."

"I've a feeling that he may have tried to and that Fleury simply wouldn't. Just refused to budge. Simply clung here like a limpet—limpets do cling?"

"I think they do. On rocks."

"Well, we'll make it a leech. It doesn't matter. Fleury remained glued simply so that he could fire broadsides of his mad notions at Justin whenever he felt like it. Justin was much too kindhearted to force the point. His sense of obligation because of that accident business seemed to increase rather than diminish."

Washburn announced dinner.

Ann continued to think of Fleury as she walked into the dining room: Are you the one? Did you kill him? Did you hate him for what he did to your arm, and did you brood yourself toward homicide because he would not underwrite your Utopia? It could be. But where was Alice in all that?

Very much in it, Ann realized as she recalled Estelle's description of Fleury's adoration of Alice "from afar." How deeply the acid could have bitten Fleury to have been changed through an accident from a personable young man into one whom he felt his adored one might have looked on with distaste.

"Yes," she said to Sergeant Hurlstone, whom she found seated at her left, "I have seen *Arsenic and Old Lace* and I liked it very much."

There was this about Sergeant Hurlstone, Ann realized: he kept things in their niches. They were at dinner, and the talk would, therefore, be the talk which he understood was suitable for talk at dinner when served as the meal was and at a place like Black Tor.

She began to like him very much. He was, he admitted, a subscriber to the Book-of-the-Month Club. He believed in a balanced mental ration as firmly as in a diet properly apportioned among the vitamins. He regretted, during the roast, that the opera seemed on its last legs.

It was different after dinner was over and he was alone with Ann, at his request, in her living room.

"Now," he said, "we can get down to work."

CHAPTER XVIII

Sergeant Hurlstone listened with his granite calm until Ann was through. She began to feel toward the close like a Scheherazade on the thousand-and-second night.

"What," he asked, when Ann had run down, "have you left out?"

"Heavens!"

His slate eyes widened in faint reproach.

"You have been here since yesterday afternoon."

"And I have talked for over an hour."

"You have told me what you discussed with Mr. Marlow, with Miss Estelle Marlow, with Mr. Appleby, and Dr. Johnson. There were others. Who?"

Ann took a fresh grip and rounded out the canvas with the pilot, the coachman, Washburn, Danning, the young man from the photography laboratory, and the recent fervid cocktail with Fleury, during which he had expounded his socialistic notions with such zest.

Sergeant Hurlstone stood up. He walked over to the desk at which Alice, according to Danning, so frequently had sat.

"Fine Adam," he said.

"You know furniture, Sergeant?"

"I try to know something about everything. Robert Adam is simple. The wreaths and paterae, the honeysuckle and that fan ornament. You can't mistake him. What interests me, Miss Marlow, is that this desk must have been built before 1792."

"Why? I mean why the interest? Do you believe that age gives a thing some psychic value? That Danning 'feels' Alice Marlow more than if the desk were modern?"

Ann had the odd impression that her question relieved him. Not the question itself, so much as her interpretation of his interest in the desk.

He said, "Why not? The psychic is a state of mind, and the mind is lulled by old things. The new excites it. You are more receptive when your mind is at rest. Take India or China. There's where you find your mystics and your true fundamentalists. Not here, with our chromium and plastics and glass."

Sergeant Hurlstone gave a parting touch to the desk's velvet patina. He returned to the fire.

He said, "We must go back to the origin of this matter. The murder of Alice Marlow. I agree with Mr. Harlan that it was a crime of impulse, instantly conceived and committed. Then do you find a paradox?"

"I can't say I do."

"Murderers are supposed to conform to a set pattern. Once a sash weight, always a sash weight; once poison, always poison. That sort of thing. Largely it's true, but here we are faced with the exception to the rule. We find increasing premeditation and more care in preparation. The hunting accident to Jerry Abbott—it had to be plotted and the proper moment waited for. The ptomaine of Frank Lawrence. Still more detail and elaboration. The radioactive substance eaten by Mr. Marlow. Great patience there and ingenuity. The murderer has developed a sharp finesse. I accept the viewpoint that all sprang from Alice Marlow's death."

"Then you must also accept the fact that Fred Marlow was innocent?"

"It would be stupid not to. The thread runs backward through twenty years. It would be equally stupid to concentrate on an original motive such as jealousy, the one accepted at the trial. Perhaps it was a crime of passion. Perhaps not."

"What else?"

"Much else. Its obviousness at the time confused the issue. Jealousy, rage, murder. So simple, and all the ingredients were at hand. Also the protagonists. Jerry Abbott, still in love with her. The jealous husband. All too neat. Look here, Miss Marlow."

"Yes, Sergeant Hurlstone?"

"Your grandfather warned you to trust no one."

"With the exception of Mr. Harlan."

"So you said. I suggest you remove the exception."

"But you can't say a thing like that without giving me a reason."

"Mr. Harlan was here at the time of Alice Marlow's murder. He was here when Jerry Abbott suffered his hunting accident. He has been here frequently during the years and was in Mr. Marlow's confidence. Such reasons are enough. I do not isolate him. I simply include him and advise you to do likewise. This will be all for tonight, Miss Marlow. Thank you very much."

Sergeant Hurlstone stood up. He moved to the door. He said before leaving, "These crimes were not conceived by a ninny."

CHAPTER XIX

The door closed on Sergeant Hurlstone.

It was nonsense, Ann thought, about Clarence Harlan. On the other hand, family lawyers had had their popular run: And so, my dears, the old counselor did it because he had a perfectly poisonous appetite for the stock market and had helped himself to fifty gilt-edged bonds from your late grandpapa's estate.

Rubbish and nonsense.

Ann looked at the time and thought she would go to bed. It was after eleven. She went through the bedroom and into the dressing room. Danning had laid her things out for the night. She took her dress off and put on a wrapper. She sat at the dressing table and began to take her face apart for the night. A quiet night, now, except for the continual pelt of raindrops against the windows. A dreary sound and a furtive one.

Bill had called up last night around this time.

What was the matter with the dope? A sterling line of Forrest forebears—no, that was absurd. "The Marlow Murder Baby." That's what Marlow had said the press had called her. Heaven knew what they were planning to call her now. Change Baby to Heiress and leave the rest? That wouldn't matter to Bill.

Her money? That might, yes. Ann knew examples—and they weren't pleasant—of a man with a very rich wife. Look at the Stuttmans. Harriet conscientiously lived down to Peter's salary, and there was Peter, feeling futile and frustrated. You could tell it. They weren't happy.

There was no earthly reason why such a setup shouldn't work out, but it so rarely, if ever, did. Never that Ann knew of. With gigolos, of course, and the handsome frameworks that you bought and paid for. But not with men like Bill. When she looked at it that way it was depressing as hell.

The dressing-room door was slightly open, and clearly in the hush and muted pelting of the rain Ann heard a small sound of something tapping once on metal. It gathered her nerves into a knot of fright.

She called out sharply: "Who's there?"

Estelle's voice said: "I am, dear."

Estelle pushed the dressing-room door wide open and came in. Her face was tired and pale, and her plump, pleasing body seemed to have lost its stiffening.

"I knocked," Estelle said, "but you didn't answer, so I came in. I thought you must be getting ready for bed." I did not hear you knock, Ann thought. You came in and clicked something against metal in the bedroom or the living room. You did not call to me as soon as you came in. You were in there doing something.

"Is there something I can do, Estelle?"

"No, dear. I just wanted to say good night."

Ann thought: What were you doing? Trust no one, Marlow said. Only Clarence Harlan. Don't even trust Harlan, Sergeant Hurlstone said.

Estelle sat down on a slipper chair. Her dimpled hands, resting quietly on her lap, were holding something. Ann thought it a small round box.

"It has been a nervous day," Estelle went on. "It seems trifling to call such a tragic day nervous, but that's what it amounts to. It's fretful on the nerves. You look worn out."

"Just a cold-cream pallor."

"No, I watched you during dinner, dear. You will need a good sleep in order to face tomorrow. I think I dread the press more than I do the officers of the law. The press can be very wearing. There's such a gusto about them. Would you like a sedative? I've some tablets I used to use in Paris. They're amazing."

"I think not, but thank you, Estelle. I never have used any."

"Amazing," Ann thought, would probably be right. A delicious coating of sugar to cover that arsenical taste. I'm being brutally unjust. Estelle came here from the kindness of her heart. It's she who needs comfort and rest. Possibly she was fond of Marlow, truly fond, and his cruel death has left her deeply, miserably shaken. Trust no one, not even Harlan, Sergeant Hurlstone said.

Was it thought transference? Because Estelle went on: "How did Sergeant Hurlstone strike you?"

"As a devastatingly intelligent and immovable force."

"He alarmed me, too, until he admitted he had taken his B.A. at Harvard. An intellectual fullback of the most admirable sort, with sidelines of dishes and ushering at concerts and things like that to help pay his expenses. He instructed me that lukewarm water is much better than cold for removing hardened eggs from china, and I sent a note down to the kitchen telling them so." Estelle leaned forward and said impulsively, "Do you know what really did frighten me about him?"

"What, Estelle?"

"He asked me nothing about Alice. It was all Justin, this immediate tragedy of ours."

"But why should that frighten you?"

Estelle said impatiently, "Surely you realize the two events are linked? I'm sensitive about eyes. I felt that all the while he was questioning me about Justin his eyes were questioning me about Alice. Or is that too Picabia?"

"Well, it's quite a stunt."

"The result was that I positively reeked with guilt. I could have walked on in any Grand Guignol production and been spotted for the villainess in a minute. He left me limp." Estelle stood up. "I'm dead. Good night, dear."

"Good night, Estelle."

Estelle looked at Ann critically before she left the room.

She said, "You look dead too."

Ann stood in the doorway until Estelle had gone through the bedroom and into the living room. She heard, because she was listening for it, the sound of the living-room door as it closed. Then she went in and turned the small knob which bolted it.

She was, she admitted, in a state. She wondered just how lightly that "You look dead too" of Estelle's was to be brushed away.

What was the click against metal she had heard? What was it that Estelle had done? The living room was calm and serene: a haven of beautiful peace. The bedroom, too, offered no metal-clicked note. Silver was a soft sheen on the bed table: the silver tray, the carafe of iced water, the glass.

Ann lifted the stopper from the carafe and cautiously sniffed. There was no odor to the water. No scent of almonds. She replaced the stopper.

There was something about the glass.

It was wet on the inside. Estelle had used it and taken a drink. It had clicked against the carafe or the tray when Estelle had put it down. That would be all right.

It could also not be all right. The carafe would have been full to the brim, and Estelle might have needed to get rid of some of the water in order to make room for a good-sized dose of narcotic or poison. The simplest way of obtaining this required room would be to pour out some of the water and drink it.

Ann went to the house phone and got Washburn.

"Do you know where Sergeant Hurlstone is?" she asked.

"I believe he is in the lounge, Miss Marlow."

"Thank you. I'll ring it and see."

She pressed the button marked Lounge. She recognized Sergeant Hurlstone's sturdy voice.

"Would you mind coming up?" she asked.

"Certainly, Miss Marlow."

Ann said when he came into the living room: "This is either very stupid of me or it's not. Estelle Marlow has just been in here to say good night. I was in the dressing room and did not hear her come in. I did hear a sound like something clicking against metal. I called out, and she came in and joined me. The drinking glass beside the carafe in the bedroom is wet on the inside. I think she took a drink of water."

Sergeant Hurlstone continued to listen in stony silence. "My nerves are none too good right now," Ann said. "It occurred to me that the best way for anyone to get rid of some of the water would be to drink it. If you wanted to put something else into the carafe in its place. Either poison or a narcotic. This is a damnable attitude to take, but you and Mr. Marlow and Mr. Harlan have all got me to a point where I don't know where I stand. I'm sick and I'm frightened about everything."

"You are not being stupid. Neither, if the water has been poisoned, was Miss Estelle Marlow. Unless you had happened to notice that the glass had just been used you could have taken a drink from the carafe, and no one would have known she had been in here."

"That's somewhat confusing."

"Not at all. It is perfectly plain. If that water is poisoned and you had drunk some you would be unable to state that Miss Marlow had just been in to see you because you would be dead."

Sergeant Hurlstone went into the bedroom. He came back carrying the silver tray with the carafe and drinking glass.

"Dr. Johnson and Dr. Bedmann are in the laboratory doing the autopsy," he said.

He went to the door.

He said, "I'll let you know."

CHAPTER XX

The moments dragged. Ten went by. They seemed ten hours. Whenever Ann had taken photographs of animals in cages her heart had always been filled with pity at their plight. But it had been an academic pity: How terrible to cage an animal. A free, wild thing born for the open spaces.

It was no longer academic. Not that she felt immoderately wild or was filled with any yearning to be set down in the heart of Texas, but she did feel caged. She wanted to get out of that house and get out soon.

She pondered escape. Prisoners were always accomplishing it and under the most adverse of circumstances. Usually through the aid of a pie in which Mother had absent-mindedly baked a steel file and some yards of rope. So far as that goes, take Houdini. Ann took him for twenty minutes. He got her no place.

I will sit down calmly, she decided, and will read a good thick book. She went to a bookcase and looked titles over. They hadn't, it was obvious, been changed since the days of Alice. Edith Wharton was gone in for heavily. Ann shuddered. That certainly would do the trick: a delicious, carefree hour spent with *Ethan Frome*. Boy!

She took off her wrapper and put on her dress. She put back her face. She walked out into the hall and took the lift down to the ground floor. She went into the lounge.

Sergeant Hurlstone was sitting near the fire in a straight-backed chair. On his lap was a large black cat.

"I couldn't stay up there alone," Ann said. "In about ten more minutes I'd have been letting my hair hang out the window and sliding down it to the ground."

She sat on the sofa and watched him stroke the cat.

"I was about to phone you, Miss Marlow. Dr. Bedmann has just completed the test. He found the water in the carafe had been poisoned. About one swallow would have been enough, he said."

Ann felt as though she had actually taken it. The jolt made her ill. It wasn't only that death had been there in the carafe but that Estelle had put it there. And then had come into the dressing room and chatted serenely away, leaving, as she said good night, that pregnant, fruitful bon mot: "You look dead too."

Ann said after a while, "Will you arrest her?"

"Miss Estelle Marlow? No. Nothing is certain. I think tomorrow we can tell. We will know better how we stand."

His fingers found the cat's neck. The cat purred contentedly with tight-shut eyes.

"This cat belongs to the cook," Sergeant Hurlstone said.

The cat stretched dark velvet legs while claws slid out from pale pads. He yawned prodigiously, then the claws went back and he pressed close to Hurlstone's flat stomach and considered sleep.

Through the shakingly shocking knowledge that one swallow of the poisoned water would have been (as Hurlstone put it) enough, Ann considered the oddity that a monolith like Hurlstone should have a tenderness for cats. A tolerant courtesy toward them would have seemed more in keeping. There was a prick of anger, too, in that he accepted her brush against a poisoned demise with such placidity. His life, she supposed somewhat bitterly, had accustomed him to taking such mordant happenstances in his stride. "Aren't you going to do anything about it at all, Sergeant Hurlstone?"

He smiled and was suddenly human and warm.

"You are annoyed. I'm not indifferent. I've sent for Danning."

"Isn't that a little farfetched? I thought that the old family retainer had been outlawed with dull thuds."

"You are still upset by my attitude. Don't be. Danning filled the carafe and left it on your bed table. That was her job. So we start with her."

Danning and the strokes of midnight coincided. At Sergeant Hurlstone's request she sat down. Ann considered that Danning's seventh-daughter proclivities were on the job again, for the woman had a look which, if not specifically astral, was at least remote.

Sergeant Hurlstone told her why he had asked her to come.

"I filled the carafe in the service pantry on the third floor," Danning said.

"Were you alone?"

"Yes. I took the carafe directly to Miss Marlow's room and put it on the bed table. That was the last I had to do with it."

"Did anyone come in while you were there?"

"No. I turned down the bed and fixed things for the night. Then I left. Mr. Thurlow was in the hallway by the lift. I said good night to him and went back to our quarters. Mr. Thurlow is the estate manager." Danning said directly to Ann: "Something was wrong with the water, wasn't it?"

"It was poisoned."

"I thought so. Sergeant Hurlstone would not have sent for me other-wise." Her voice acquired a definite quiver. "Death favors some houses, I think. Deaths by violence." The quiver accelerated to a chilling degree. "Leave here, Miss Marlow. Don't come back again until the place is cleansed. I feel it's evil here. Evil for you." Danning made a helpless gesture of apology for having said this.

Her face was completely pale, and light beads of sweat damped its skin. "Please don't mind my talking to you like this."

Ann did mind, in a fashion. The quiver had injected an almost con-juring quality into Danning's voice. It brought the dead Marlow back into the shadowed room, the strong essence of him distilled from the sadness of his lifetime and the cruelty of his leaving.

Alice and Fred and the others came too. And one more. The one who had killed them all. The agile one who skipped from knives to guns to poisons in their lethally infinite variety. Whose busy brain would now be busier still.

A rush of hatred came to Ann for this evil one. She thought of him as a monster, comfortable in human shape, eating and drinking and viewing the good things in life. An egocentric slug, perhaps with charm, whose vicious brain selected deaths with delicacy and meted them out.

The hatred was so sudden and so vast that it swept out personal fear, and Ann Ledrick died. She became Ann Marlow. Those people who had been killed were her people. Justin Marlow, whose life had been turned into a living hell through the machinations of this wicked person, be-came her grandfather and no longer just a rich man's name. If she were to betray him he would have died in vain. Ann thought of it as exactly that and found no grandiloquence in the phrasing.

"I had thought of leaving for New York tomorrow," she said. "But I am not. I am staying here."

The firm edge to Ann's voice brought Danning reluctantly back from her protoplasmic fields.

"Yes, yes, of course, Miss Marlow. Can I be of any further help, Sergeant Hurlstone?"

"You can. I shall make a statement. Tell me the first thing that comes into your mind. Don't stop to consider. Just come right out with it."

"Very well, Sergeant."

"Alice Marlow's murder."

"Chin."

"Good. Now what's the connection?"

"Chin was her chow puppy. Chin had cut her foot in the morning, and Dr. Johnson had treated it and bandaged it up. Mrs. Marlow carried

Chin to the music room with her after lunch and put her on a cushioned stool near the spinet. That was the day she was killed."

"How do you know she did?"

"Mr. Washburn told me so afterward. When Mr. Fleury yelled murder the way he did and the word got around to the servants' quarters I ran to the music room, and Chin was still on the stool. She was trembling and made awful sounds. Little ones. That's why, when I think back, I always think first of Chin."

"What other things come to you?"

"Blood, and Mr. Fred sick and white as a sheet, and Mr. Frank Lawrence seeming stunned, and the bitter look on Mr. Jerry Abbott's face, like somebody had reached a hand inside and twisted him. Mr. Appleby held his arms. Mr. Appleby was much stronger than Mr. Abbott and easily kept him from killing Mr. Fred."

"Why do you say that?"

"Because Mr. Abbott said he was going to beat the life out of him."

"I understood that Mr. Appleby was down in the entrance hall. That he had just come indoors from the storm."

"He had, but he ran upstairs with Mr. Washburn, and they were both in the music room when I got there. Then Mr. Marlow came in, and it was all the child, of course. You, Miss Marlow. Sending for Dr. Johnson and everything done that you might be delivered, and you were, and it was a miracle."

"Those are the general things," Sergeant Hurlstone said. "Give me some others, such as Chin."

Danning grew remote again. Her eyes lost focus.

"The desk, maybe."

"Yes?"

"The desk where she wrote her poetry. She was so neat about things. If she opened a drawer she closed it. The drawer where she kept her private letters was not quite closed. I had gone to her rooms to see that they were in order and to cry."

"Did you tell anyone about the drawer?"

"I told the troopers and Mr. Harlan and Mr. Marlow. The troopers went through the letters, and one of them was used at the trial, one that Mr. Abbott had written, saying he would never stop loving her."

"I know about that letter. I did not know about the half-opened drawer. Anything else?"

"No, just Chin and the desk drawer."

"You have helped me. Thank you. Good night, Danning."

Sergeant Hurlstone stood up. He did so carefully and without disturbing the calm repose of the dark cat. He settled the cat on the seat of the chair. He went to the house telephone. He was connected through the estate's private exchange with the house of the manager, Martin Thurlow.

"Will there be anything further I can do for you tonight, Miss Marlow?" Danning asked.

"No, thank you. Good night, Danning."

"Good night, Miss Marlow. Let us hope."

With this cryptic utterance Danning walked away, and Ann studied her retreating back. A maid's white uniform. What was it Harlan had said? The back which Ludwig Appleby had seen—it wasn't a shirt, or a coat, or a dress. There was something unique about it.

A white uniform?

Danning?

Why Danning?

CHAPTER XXI

Sergeant Hurlstone returned to his chair and settled the cat on his lap. The cat stayed pleased.

"What got into you, Miss Marlow, when Danning turned the heat on about wanting you to leave here?"

"I got mad."

"I thought you were."

"I'm going to fight this the way Mr. Marlow fought it."

"Glad you feel that way."

"Why did the dog interest you, and the desk drawer?"

"The dog saw the crime committed. Chows are jealous of their masters. Did she leap upon the attacker? Tear at him with her teeth? There are no records of torn clothes or of flesh lacerations. No. The dog trembled on her cushion and made little noises. That's odd business for a chow. As for the desk drawer, they took it for granted."

"How for granted?"

"That the drawer had been opened and gone through before the crime. It was brought out by the prosecution that Abbott's letter was still in the drawer when the troopers searched it. It was claimed that Abbott would have destroyed the letter if it were he who had looked through the drawer. They said Fred Marlow opened the drawer and found the letter, that he read it, went mad, and rushed down to the music room and killed her."

"Well?"

"I don't take any of that for granted. In the first place, a guy in that frame of mind would have taken the letter down with him and brandished it at her. And in the second place, the drawer could have been searched after Alice Marlow was killed, not before. It could have been searched between the times when the murderer stabbed her and when Danning found the drawer half closed. Abbott's letter might well have had nothing to do with it. I have asked Mr. Thurlow to come here. He is our next link in the carafe."

Sergeant Hurlstone stoically began to brood, and Ann was getting fed up—in fact, stuffed—with it. An absolute hush settled down on the large room. There was warmth from the fire, but it did not warm her. Her pique reached anger. Ice. She was conscious that Sergeant Hurlstone's Olympian indifference was not, basically, indifference at all, that it was the confidence of a trained and intelligent man whose feet were planted on the right track.

But after all...

After all, nothing but the sharpest sort of wit had saved her from a toxic demise. Her wit. Surely it deserved some pinch of official commendation: How clever you were, Miss Marlow, not to die. Some flick of oral joy that that eventuality had not occurred, some trust, some assurance that she would be guarded against such hidden and venomous fangs in the future. But no.

"You know where you're going," she said shortly. "One trusts."

"I think I do."

"There is nothing so exasperating as the white-rabbit trick, Sergeant Hurlstone."

"There is nothing so embarrassing or so stupid as pulling one out of a hat and finding it's the wrong one. I will tell you this. I want motive. I want the precise motive as to why Alice Marlow was killed. Passion, jealousy, fear, hate, money, revenge. That's about the general list. Which? We can settle on none of them and rule none of them out." He looked toward the distant doorway. He said, "Come in, Mr. Thurlow."

Martin Thurlow joined them with precise and measured steps. Firelight caromed from the lenses of his rimless glasses and laced small lusters through his thinning hair. He bowed and smiled with reserved precision to Ann. He sat down.

Sergeant Hurlstone came directly to the point.

"You were standing by the elevator door, Mr. Thurlow, when Danning came into the hallway from Miss Marlow's room. This was just a short while ago. She said good night to you."

"Yes, that is correct."

"Where had you been, please?"

"Mr. Fleury and I were in conference with Miss Estelle Marlow in her living room. Mr. Fleury remained with her to take notes on arrangements concerning the funeral. I left. The lift was in operation when Danning wished me good night. It stopped at the third floor, and Mr. Appleby came out."

"Did he mention where he was going?"

"No, and I did not inquire. I presume he was going to his rooms to retire for the night. I took the lift down and went to my house."

"You have been here for about fifteen years, Mr. Thurlow?"

"That is correct."

"Had Mr. Marlow known you before you came? How did he happen to get in touch with you?"

"I had been the manager of Mrs. Walter McFraney's estate at Mount Desert. After her death I was without a post. Mr. Clarence Harlan knew of this. He knew about me. He recommended me to Mr. Marlow."

"You were here at the time when two men were drowned in Crystal Lake. Lattigan and Turfmann, both employees. Do you remember the details?"

"I remember very well. Both of them were old hands. They had been in service here for years and were good men. They took care of the greenhouses. Lattigan had just bought a canoe rigged for sailing. He took Turfmann out with him that Sunday. There was a squall and the canoe overturned. They could swim, but not well enough. Panic and the icy water, I suppose. That was the end of them."

"While they were under you did either of them ever refer to Mrs. Marlow's death?"

"No."

Sergeant Hurlstone then said with no change of pace: "At whose suggestion was luminous paint used to band the trees as a black-out precaution?"

"I wondered when that would occur to you." Thurlow thawed visibly and smiled. "It was my suggestion. I ordered the paint somewhat over a year ago, when it was first indicated that black-outs would be required. The paint is composed of eight parts zinc pyrosulphide and one part of a radioactive substance called radiothorium. I presume you have settled on the paint as the medium for Mr. Marlow's radium poisoning? I have."

"I have settled on nothing."

"Then you are a uniquely clever man. I accept the paint as the obvious, as having been handy. The storehouse for the estate's supplies is reasonably accessible during the daytime to anyone. In an isolated and socially insular community such as Black Tor there is no incentive for petty thievery. I should think that one drop of the luminous paint would have been enough. You have a hard row to hoe, Sergeant Hurlstone."

"I know it."

"You like cats, I see."

Sergeant Hurlstone regarded Thurlow steadily. His strong fingers were gentle on the cat's dark fur.

"Yes," he said. "I do."

"That is interesting. I should have laid odds on the reverse." Thurlow stood up and started to say good night. He hesitated. "Would you mind telling me why this questioning about my standing before the lift and Danning having seen me there?"

"She had just left a carafe of water in Miss Marlow's room. The water was poisoned."

Thurlow displayed no particular sense of shock. He thought it over for a moment.

"Yes," he said to Ann, "that is understandable. Naturally you must expect things like that."

CHAPTER XXII

"The man," Ann said, "is a machine."

"Mr. Thurlow?"

"Yes. He has probably projected my graph, or whatever that thing is that jerks up and down and shows the rise and fall of stocks. Each peak a nice fresh brush with violent death."

Hurlstone smiled fractionally.

"He struck me as smart."

"That is both soothing, Sergeant Hurlstone, and a big help. It's a wonder to me the administration hasn't snatched you up to be the czar of public morale. Did Mr. Thurlow also strike you as a fit subject for the suspect list?"

"No. Why should he have? He wasn't here when Alice Marlow was killed."

"Need he have been? He might have known her in Boston."

"He might. What of it? There are no secret passages or trap doors in this house that I know of. He would have had to be here in order to stab her. If he had been here he would have been seen."

"I was stupid. My mind is turning into an octopus. Tentacles reaching all over the place. Hundreds of them."

"Eight," Hurlstone said dispassionately. "An octopus is an eight-armed cephalopod."

Ann honestly thought she would have slapped him if Ludwig hadn't come in. A lounging jacket of wine-colored faille with rather startling lapels and that this-ought-to-get-them look had replaced Ludwig's dinner coat. And, Ann decided, it wasn't a Christmas present.

The contrast between Ludwig and Sergeant Hurlstone caught her. If Ludwig could strip off twenty years it possibly would not have been so acute. There was little more fatal to he-men than beginning, like Ludwig, to be lightly larded by the forties.

She watched him consciously holding in a crescent middle and his manner of going Sergeant Hurlstone one better as he, too, took a sitting stance in a straight-backed chair. A good wave of scotch whisky radiated out from him, and he was, Ann decided, well away on his second leg toward oblivion.

"I suppose," Ludwig said graciously to both of them, "you've cooked me up between you. I could hear the bracelets rattling in your voice when you phoned, Sergeant."

Sergeant Hurlstone's facade reflected none of Ludwig's affability.

"They're still in my pocket, Mr. Appleby."

"Forgive me if I insist that the impression still remains. Your voice is at bailiff pitch." Ludwig was studying Ann curiously. "What has happened to you, Ann? You've lost that dewy and, if I may say so, blankish look. Your face is vitally grim."

"I feel grim, Ludwig. And also vital."

"Excellent. The Marlow mantle is being donned. Why did you send for me, Sergeant Hurlstone? Is this a where-were-you-when? "

"Yes, you can call it so. Mr. Thurlow was waiting to take the lift when you stepped out of it. This was on the third floor and just a short while ago. Do you confirm that?"

"Confirm? I do. You seem rather serious for such a casual event. Has something happened recently? Something deadly, of course?" Ludwig's dark, bold eyes settled on Ann. "To you?"

"The water in Miss Marlow's carafe was poisoned," Sergeant Hurlstone said.

Ludwig did a splendid job at blanching. His lush lips parted slightly in astounded shock. His hairy fingers clutched his knees. A Rodin figure registering Aghast.

"When," he said mellowly, "will this end? Has Dr. Johnson treated you? I've always understood that poisoned people twisted up into knots. You look perfectly all right, Ann."

"I am all right. I didn't drink any."

Ludwig evidently decided he had blanched enough. He said with the sharpest sort of curiosity, "Then how did you know the water was poisoned?"

"That," Sergeant Hurlstone said, "is a story which can be deferred. Tell me this, Mr. Appleby. Did you see Mr. Thurlow go into the lift and close the door?"

"No, but I heard it close. It makes that unique, soft clashing effect. Like the aftermath of a banana peel. I was walking toward my room." Ludwig's lively air of speculation increased. "Surely not Thurlow? He's only been here about fifteen years. Simply vats of money to dig his fingers in. Stop me if my eyes begin to glitter."

"Did you go directly to your rooms and stay in them?"

"I went to them, yes. I did not stay in them. And I did not collect a dose of poison from my cache under a bathroom tile and skulk with it to

Ann's carafe." Sergeant Hurlstone permitted the dark cat lazily to shift its position.

"What was it you did do, Mr. Appleby?"

Ludwig's sudden air of sober candor was admirable. "You know, this may mean something. I was on my way to see Estelle. Fleury was standing in front of your door, Ann. He had either knocked or was just about to. Fleury. Now there's a thought. I never considered Fleury. I've always expected him to blow his top at any minute, but I never considered him seriously with murder."

"Did Fleury see you?" Sergeant Hurlstone asked.

"I don't imagine he did. His back was toward me, and he was at the end of that long hall. Why on earth don't you ask him? I'll phone him to come down. Shall I?"

"Thank you."

Ludwig said, after he came back from the house phone, "This fits in with the things I told you during cocktails, Ann."

Sergeant Hurlstone looked at Ann reproachfully.

He said, "What were they, Mr. Appleby?"

"Oh, just about Fleury being a fanatic. About my having advised Justin again and again to get rid of him. You know, the more I think of it, the better I like it. He was crazy about Alice. We used to kid her a little about it."

"Just how crazy would you say?"

"Well, in a Byronic, terribly high-plane sort of way. Would that fit Byron? I don't know."

"Sergeant Hurlstone," Ann said bitterly, "will." Hurlstone did. He quoted with precision the young Byron's remark that his school friendships were, with him, passions. He touched with disfavor on the young man's habit of lying down and dreaming on his favorite tombstone in the churchyard and his love for his distant relative, Alary Ann Chatworth, who made him shortly realize the hopelessness of his passion and threw him out alone on a wide, wide sea. Yes, Hurlstone said, you might call Fleury's attitude toward Alice Marlow as Byronic.

"Well, I," Ludwig said, "will be damned. And it will be a long, long day before I start anything like that again. Look here, here's another point. Fleury's the one who walked in and saw Fred standing there with the knife. Why couldn't that have been a return walk? Like that thing they used to do on the stage when the army marched by? I mean he could have stabbed Alice and gone away and then have been drawn back by remorse, only to see Fred with the knife. Naturally he grabbed it as an out and yelled murder."

"Aren't you forgetting the famous 'white back,' Mr. Appleby? The one you yourself saw in the music-room window?"

Ludwig did not deflate. He looked smug and a little bit cunning.

"You couldn't, of course, know how Fleury looked back then. Or how he acted, as a matter of fact. Not one of us would have been surprised if he had turned up, some morning for breakfast, in a sheet."

CHAPTER XXIII

Fleury was no help at all. He admitted candidly that he had stood for a while before Ann's door and had been of two minds about knocking. The second mind (the not-to-knock one) had conquered. His Utopian urges had continued to obsess him, and they had lingered even through the conference with Thurlow and Estelle.

Obviously he considered Ann as offering more fallow ground for socialistic seedlings than her grandfather had offered, but the lateness of the hour had eventually deterred him. Also, the more practical fact that she was probably in bed.

So there, Ann thought, they were. Not one of them who could not have slipped inside her bedroom and concocted the deadly dose. She wondered what the poison had been. Odorless, because she had sniffed. Probably tasteless too. Although one swallow might have been managed before being repelled by a flavor. She would ask Sergeant Hurlstone after this relay of suspects abated.

Truly a relay in that each had put the finger on his successor. A lot of trick timing there, unless one were a liar.

It wasn't very tricky at that, though. Thurlow and Fleury had been with Estelle, and Fleury had lingered to pothook funeral arrangements in his notebook. Ludwig's having stepped out of the lift just as Thurlow was desirous of stepping into it was the only coincidental thing. Although his stepping out into the hallway just when Fleury had finished with Estelle and was hovering before Ann's door had been coincidental too.

There was a lot coincidental about Ludwig.

Twenty years ago he had happened to glance up at the music-room windows just as Alice was being murdered and had glimpsed the almost identifiable white back. Possibly a coincidence carrier, like Typhoid Mary. Possibly, quite possibly, the murderer.

Piqued passion would be the motive if he were. If Alice (who had been so devastating and so coveted) had failed to fall for Ludwig's Tarzanish caperings and turned him down. Ann held the thoroughly feministic viewpoint that a man could be fully as deadly as a woman scorned.

What about Ludwig's wet-clothes alibi? The house was a hotel in the sense of having any number of entrances and exits. Practically a furtive character's dream home. And no one as yet had made the least mention of how long Alice had been dead when Fleury started his yells. It could have been ten or fifteen minutes or conceivably longer.

Plenty of time for Ludwig to have killed her and then hustle down a back stairway and run outside to freshen or acquire his storm-soaked condition. She retained "acquire" because there was nothing to prove that she knew of that Ludwig, after his publicized exit to breast the storm, could not have come right back indoors, changed his wet clothes, killed Alice, and then have gone out and got thoroughly soaked again.

Let it still remain a crime of impulse instantly conceived. Ludwig's rain-streaming entrance could have been cooked up after the knife had struck home. That was just as good a possibility as Sergeant Hurlstone's contention that Alice's desk drawer could have been searched and left half open after, rather than before, the murder.

No, Ann decided, you are far from being off the list, Ludwig, despite your wet-clothes entrance and your gainful vision of an odd white back. That would be something. Not only to get away with a murder for scorned passion but to cash in on it as well for years afterward. And on the outrageous presumption that Ludwig, himself the murderer, knew a clue which would indicate who the murderer was.

Ann looked at Ludwig with a moment's respect.

Ludwig's face was pleated in gourmet and bibulous lines while he listened to Fleury conclude a tirade from the saddle of his pet hobby-horse, that everyone except invalids and the very old should attend to his own menial tasks himself.

They, Fleury was saying with a conviction so hot that his words became fused, were the true leveler. Turn a tycoon or a duchess loose with a dishpan, and class consciousness would shortly melt. Ludwig amiably pointed out that so would the stock of dishes.

Ann had the feeling that Fleury would keep this up all night. Sergeant Hurlstone seemed not to mind. His eyes were open, but he was as somnolent as the dark-haired cat on his lap. But it did stop. Ludwig's amiable crack evidently upset Fleury dreadfully, because the eager light died from his eyes, and he said that if he could be of no further service he would retire to his chambers.

Ann liked the chambers touch and felt sorry for him. Sorry for his twisted arm and his good but twisted dreams. They weren't for this world of greed and slaughter. Just a dreamland for Fleury and the handful of thwarted visionaries like him to think it would be nice to live in. Meanwhile, they either washed other people's dishes or starved.

She said, when she said good night to Fleury, that they must talk again soon. He accepted the implied promise gratefully and went away looking a little less unhappy. The change was growing more complete, Ann thought. The Marlow wealth, her wealth, was now an entity in her possession. Its amount the staggering Golconda which Estelle had so rapaciously spread out before her. She was getting the feel of it.

Estelle had been right, even if the slant were not the same. All of the things in this world that she might want to possess or to do were surely possible to her, and something could be done for Fleury and his small, unhappy band of fellow travelers whose only true chance lay in a second miracle from the Mount. Something beyond the legacy which Marlow had left him. Even a token miracle, if this wealth which now was hers could so arrange it, would take the harsh edge off their lifetimes.

"You'll be a fool to fall for him," Ludwig said, having admirably followed her train of thought. "In fact, every crackpot in the country will be after you now. Justin learned how to deal with them, and you will in time."

Possibly that, also, was true. There was a law to the management of wealth, a natural law inherent in the money itself. Otherwise its power turned into defeat. "The gods, to avenge themselves, grant us our desires."

They might even grant her Bill.

And how would that turn out? A dimming Bill, ever going about his job each day after the war was over, with his earning capacity a drop in the Marlow bucket of gold. For Bill would never stop working. Work that would be a daily farce in its pretentious sense of supporting his wife.

Bill would find difficulty in looking at her, and when they no longer could look at each other equally and frankly that would be the end of it. If it wasn't already over even before it had begun. It was one o'clock in the morning, and still Bill hadn't called.

"Well," Ludwig was saying to Sergeant Hurlstone, "what about it? Does Fleury split a bracelet with me? Just take a good look at the angles."

"I looked," Sergeant Hurlstone said.

CHAPTER XXIV

Dr. Johnson came toward them from the distant doorway. A man was with him, and Ann supposed he would be Medical Examiner Bedmann. They both looked tired. The man was Dr. Bedmann, and Dr. Johnson introduced him.

Dr. Bedmann was young, and Ann thought he must be of the age that Dr. Johnson was when Alice had been killed. Under his tired look there was an eager one which searched beyond any present moment and into the future. She found herself slipping naturally into the role of hostess and suggested drinks. Ludwig was enthusiastically enchanted with this. He went over and pressed a button for Washburn.

"Well," Dr. Johnson said, "it's over. It's done. I took the liberty of telephoning Miss Marlow that we were finished with the autopsy, Sergeant Hurlstone. She will join us down here."

Estelle's arrival was shortly followed by Washburn with the drinks. Marlow, Dr. Johnson said, had had his death hastened beyond the radioactive poisoning in a manner which the autopsy had clearly shown. Dr. Johnson tried obviously for Estelle's sake and for Ann's to gloss the more repellent features of the job which he and Dr. Bedmann had done.

He told them that pyrogallol was the agent that had accomplished the trick. A white and odorless crystalline powder. Its form was of leaflets or of needles that were very fine. He offered this strange sop of glossing in a distorted stab at beautifying the crystals' vicious powers of death.

In Marlow's case the pyrogallol had presented one of its rare performances of causing embolism, having degenerated Marlow's erythrocytes, a term which Dr. Johnson himself degenerated into the more comprehensible one of red blood corpuscles. The reddish-brown blood coagula had put Dr. Bedmann and himself rapidly on the track.

The fatal dose for this beautiful but unhappily toxic crystalline could vary from 4.9 grams to 20 grams, and Marlow had been especially ripe for its evil results, in that age and disease had rendered his susceptibility to the poison most acute.

With Ann, he said, death would have been longer in coming. Possibly a few days. And the clinical picture would, among other unpleasant symptoms, have offered cyanosis and chills. Then death would have reached her by collapse.

Yes, the poison was the same. It had hurried off Marlow and it had been introduced into the water of Ann's carafe.

Estelle was sitting beside Ann on the sofa. The slow, drawn, ghastly sound which her breath made was like nothing which Ann had ever heard before. Almost a death rattle, Ann supposed, could be like it. Estelle's voice, when she spoke, had a choking moisture in it, a burbling sound as when water is drawn into the lungs.

"Why wasn't I told? What is this, Ann?"

Dr. Johnson saved her from fainting. He soothed her, calmed her, and dosed her with a pill while the water-carafe business was explained to her. Estelle was convincingly superb about it, almost frighteningly so, and Ann handed it a mental Oscar as certainly being the best performance of the year. She did this with complete callousness and a hardening of her heart, Dr. Johnson's calm portrayal of, among other unpleasant symptoms, cyanosis and chills and a death by collapse still being urgent with her. All in one swallow.

Dr. Johnson went on to say, after Estelle was breathing normally again, that pyrogallol was accessible to anyone on the place who cared to avail himself of the photography laboratory. Its use in photography was as a reducing agent. Harley Brown, who was in charge of the laboratory, had told them that pyrogallol was always kept in stock.

As for the long-range plan to efface Marlow through a radioactive substance, further unpleasantness faced them there. Dr. Johnson was sorry there could be no choice. He did not, he said, know what plans were in mind for the funeral, but whatever they were, the body would have to be cremated.

The post-mortem test for such radium poisoning required that the bone ash and the ash of certain organs which he did not enumerate be placed in a dark room on photographic film, wrapped and sealed in black opaque paper. This would have to be gone through with as an official gesture, in spite of the fact that Miss Ann Marlow's chance catching of the silvery bones on her pictures of the ocelots left no doubts as to what the results would be.

Estelle's dimpled hands were now lifeless on the rose velvet of the robe in which she was swathed. Although her breathing was quite under control she was apparently at a loss, for the first time in her life, for anything to say and certainly did not present her reputed portrait as one of the sights of Paris. She looked dumpy and middle-aged and tired to the point of being washed out.

She said at last: "Sergeant Hurlstone, we continue in your hands. You have been courteous and most kind. Your training and your intellect will rid Black Tor of its evil. We are at your disposal."

Sergeant Hurlstone soothed a movement of the dark-haired cat. He suggested that Ludwig and Dr. Johnson and Dr. Bedmann must all be weary and might care to retire: a suggestion which carried the implication he would be pleased if Estelle and Ann were to remain. Both doctors took the nakedly virile hint with good grace and said their good nights. They left.

Not so Ludwig.

"It will take a warrant to put me to bed, Sergeant."

"Nobody wants you to go to bed, Mr. Appleby. I am suggesting that I prefer to speak with both Miss Marlows without your being here."

"That I inferred."

"Don't be difficult, Ludwig," Estelle said. "I think temperament would be the camel's straw for me tonight."

"Very well."

Ludwig grew icily polite. His good nights were ceremonious to the point of insult.

"Sergeant Hurlstone," Estelle said after Ludwig had left the room, "you are interested in how the poison was put into the carafe. I do not know what to say, Ann, except that I did not do it. I am not ignorant of chemistry. I know that pyrogallol belongs to the corrosives, and although it is odorless, it is said to have a bitter taste. I think you will find, Sergeant Hurlstone, that it was given Justin in his blackberry brandy. Perhaps you have tasted that concoction?"

"I have. I don't like it."

"Neither do I. Justin himself considered it a palatal affront, but he favored it as a simple for his stomach. My own opinion is that anything added to it, even a bitter tang, would cause pleasure rather than alarm. I can help you to this extent. The pyrogallol was added either during a short moment when I was with Ann in her dressing room, or it was put in after I had gone."

"How long were you in the dressing room?"

"Several minutes, I believe. I suggested a sedative. We didn't say much. Do you remember, Ann?"

"It was short, Estelle."

"Yes, but it was long enough for someone to have slipped into the bedroom and put the poison in the carafe. The water was all right up until the time I went into the dressing room, because I had taken a drink of it. There was no bitter taste. That will help you, Sergeant Hurlstone, if you will believe that I am telling the truth. Otherwise you will decide that I put the poison in after having taken the drink."

Estelle started to cry. She said, "Ann—Ann, my dear, don't think this thing of me!" Her tears went beyond control.

Sergeant Hurlstone remained impassive. So did the cat, beyond opening its eyes to observe Estelle's not inconsiderable commotion and then closing them again: a human nonsensicality quite out of its feline interests or province.

Ann did her best. She encircled Estelle's plumpness and gave it a reassuring squeeze, even though thinking as she did so: This could be the wicked one, the monster who had selected apple cheeks and milk-soft skin for its disguise.

Right then it did not matter. The pressing business was to dam the flood. It subsided in time, and Estelle said, "It's Justin who upsets me too. I was fond of Justin. He and I were the last of us, Ann. Except for you."

One swallow, Ann thought, and *you* would have been the last of us, Estelle. With me dead, the Marlow fortune would have been yours. You intimated that when you told me about Marlow's will. How much did the Germans take from you of your personal wealth? How much had you left when you came back here? How much, really, is that trust fund which Marlow left you? Enough? You claim it is. But is it?

That was all right for Marlow's death and for Ann's intended one, but why had Estelle killed Alice? Weren't her riches enough even back in those days? Still, even with Alice and Fred out of the way, and with Marlow en route via his radioactive poisoning, there still, Ann considered, would remain Ann. Was that why Estelle had chosen to do Marlow in by long range? Did she hope that before the radium did the trick she could worm from Marlow the secret of Ann's hidden whereabouts?

The pattern obtained. Marlow had told Estelle only recently of the Ledrick haven and guise. And then how pursuantly the pyrogallol had been employed for a dual ending to finish it all up. Leaving Estelle with her ocelots and emeralds and, of course, millions and millions to boot.

Sergeant Hurlstone was saying: "Why did you take that drink of water from the carafe, Miss Marlow?" Estelle dabbed at tears and looked stricken. She did not answer right away. When she did so her voice held a note of reserved dignity.

"Very well, Sergeant Hurlstone. You continue in doubt. You do not believe me. I had taken a sedative before leaving my room. The wafer capsules are large. The French have a habit of aggrandizement with some of their remedies. I suppose because it makes the purchaser think he is getting his money's worth. An essential requisite in France. The cachet had left a sharp irritation in my throat which I relieved, when I reached Ann's bedroom, by taking the drink of water."

"My doubts and my beliefs or disbeliefs form the basis of my stock in trade. They are impersonal. I would be of small service to you here without them."

Estelle stood up.

"I should have realized so. With your permission I will retire, Sergeant Hurlstone."

Sergeant Hurlstone managed expertly (because of the cat) to stand up too. He said that it was entirely agreeable to him if Estelle wanted to go to bed. He wished her sound sleep.

Estelle made a motion to kiss Ann good night and then drew back. You might, her manner said, not care to have me kiss you. Ann also had stood up. Impulsively she placed a warm kiss on Estelle's pale cheek.

Tears sprang again into Estelle's eyes, and it took a second or so for her to gain control of her voice.

"The storm is over, Ann. I saw from my window a break in the night sky. There are three stars quite clear in the west. That means the end of it. The planes are under your orders. You may leave the dangers of this unhappy house when you wish. There are standing arrangements with the authorities covering civilian flights to and from Black Tor. The formalities can be attended to within an hour."

"I am staying here, Estelle."

Estelle drew a quiet breath. She did not look at Ann.

"The planes are quite safe, my dear."

"I did not mean *that*."

"It is difficult, placed as I am, to know. Thank you, Ann, for kissing me. The day will come when I shall have your trust. We will be friends."

Estelle left them then: an odd little bundle of rose velvet plumpness which was neither odd nor funny. There was too much of sound dignity in it.

"It's getting on," Sergeant Hurlstone said. "We'll go up now, and you'll get to bed."

"I couldn't sleep."

"You will sleep perfectly well, Miss Marlow. I am spending the night in your living room."

CHAPTER XXV

Some things you could not leave too long. Gaps, in time, became impossible to bridge. Bill definitely was laying off or he would have called by now. Ann had no knowledge of his phone number beyond the hotel in Washington where he had been staying. It seemed unlikely he would still be there. Surely barrack pallets were requisite hardeners for marines, not hostelries with inner springs and down. Plenty good for him, too, if he intended being tough about things.

Sergeant Hurlstone waited while she went into the small room and telephoned. The night clerk at the Washington hotel was sorry. Mr. Forrest had checked out late in the afternoon. There was a faint shock of affront in his voice at the thought that he would give a member of the armed forces' forwarding address, even if he could.

Ann was not impressed. She doubted whether the war effort would collapse if she were told what barracks or camp Bill could be found in. Although even if she did know it she couldn't call him in the middle of the night while surrounded by the frog chorus of his buddies. Not, that is, and live.

She called Fanny's apartment. Glorious, Fanny's colored maid, suggested the River Club, so she called the River Club, and after a while Fanny's voice screamed at her: "Hello, darling, what now? You're the talk of the town. Prince Oublevik wants to marry you. He's that tall, thin thing with three saber slashes and those decayed-spaniel eyes. Do you want him, dear? He's outside on the balcony eating borsch."

"No, I'll just put his name down, Fanny. I wanted to ask if you know how I can get in touch with Bill."

"Oh." There was a lull in the screaming. "So Bill hasn't called you?"

"No."

"He's a louse. He called me around dinnertime." The screaming gathered momentum again. "Take Oublevik. He's lost his castles in Bavaria—I think it's Bavaria—but he's got stunning memories of them. Gobelins for slip covers, that sort of thing. You need some tag like Princess to go with all that money. Seriously, darling, I don't know how you can reach Bill."

"Did he say anything about me when he called you?"

"He asked if I thought you were all right, and I told him that your voice had sounded plushly virile, and then—oh, *darling*, he just said, 'Thank you,' and hung up. You may as well face it. I could almost hear his neck stiffening. You'll never land him now."

"Yes, I will."

"Then you're a better minx than I think you are. My God, you're not going to *refuse* the Marlow gold pile, are you?"

"Of course not."

"You had me worried. Look, darling, there's that rum keg in Washington he used to toss pots in, and even the marines have their nights out. It's name was Fricka's—no, Freska's. I give it to you for what it may be worth. He used it for crash dives."

"Thanks, Fanny. I'll try it."

Ann said good-by. It was kind of Fanny not to ask things. Her life was a swelter of anxiety to get the news before it even was printed. This aptitude formed her bread and meat. Ann left it to long-distance to get her Freska's, and the voice that eventually greeted her was something in the neighborhood, she thought, of impure Arabian.

"Will you find out, please," Ann said, "if Mr. Bill Forrest is there?"

"Yes, yes, he is here. Very happy. All the time cry."

"Ask him to come to the phone, please."

A pause lengthened. He knows it's I, Ann decided. He's probably potted above the Plimsoll mark. Drowning his sorrows and starching the old Forrest sterling self-sufficiency.

"He says," said the odd voice, "who you are and what do you want?"

"Tell him," Ann said coldly, "I am a dying aunt."

"You wait."

"Hello, Ann," Bill's voice said shortly. (Stuffiest voice, Ann thought, I ever heard in my life.) "I called Fanny and she said you were all right."

"So she just told me. And how are you, Bill?"

"I am A-1."

"Don't boast. I just wanted to check on our date for Friday. To let you know I'd be in town."

"Oh. I'm sorry about that. The leave is off. They're just giving me tomorrow to clear up some stuff at the office. Look, Ann, about that gag I pulled. You've probably forgotten it already. About our ordering the orange blossoms on Friday, I mean. You know how we used to kid?"

"Oh, stop being so damned desperate, Bill. I wouldn't think of holding you to it."

"Holding *me* to it?"

"Naturally you have to think of your Army career. Any blot on it—"

"What blot?"

"Oh, I know. I understand." Ann sent (she hoped) a sigh along the wire. She pulled out the proper stop to give her voice, if not exactly *treviolo*, at least a wistful note. "And in any case I couldn't bear the thought of your going Over There as a widower."

"Widower? What in heaven's name are you talking about?"

"They put poison in my drinking water two hours ago. Pyrogallol, to be exact. A swallow results in cyanosis and chills, then death from collapse. It was probably a leftover from the dose they used to kill Mr. Marlow." Ann shoved back *tremolo* and replaced it with chilled steel. "The next time they'll cook up something fresh."

"*Ann!* …Ann?"

It was Ann, this time, who let the telephone go bang. She rang the estate operator and asked that no calls originating in Washington be put through to her until morning. She joined Sergeant Hurlstone.

She said: "I've just been jilted."

Sergeant Hurlstone's rocklike face again warmed faintly under a smile as they went toward the lift.

"Is this new money of yours in the way?"

"It is. Temporarily."

"I can see how he feels about it."

"You men make me sick. All of you."

"No, we don't."

"I think I'll become a princess. Princess Oublevik. I can buy a tiara and serve melted pearls in the borsch."

"You've got it bad all right."

"Are you taking that cat up with you?"

"Yes."

"What *is* this, anyhow?"

"I just like cats."

"Just as you say, Sergeant Hurlstone."

Sergeant Hurlstone pressed the button marked 3.

"Is he in the Army?"

"He is a freshly laid marine."

"I'm getting in next month."

"That leaves me nothing but to join the WAVEs."

"What have you done so far?"

"Red Cross. USO. Whatever I could."

"It won't be so very long now before you can do plenty."

They went into her living room.

The lights were on, and Estelle was seated near the coal fire which had been freshly arranged.

Estelle said, "I took the liberty of coming in, Ann. I felt that I couldn't sleep without doing at least a little toward effacing such suspicions as you may have about me. I am glad, Sergeant Hurlstone, that you, also, are here. Do you mind, Ann dear?"

"I'm only too glad, Estelle."

Sergeant Hurlstone waited until Ann sat down and then deposited himself and the dark-haired cat in an armchair. He remained courteously interested but completely removed, and his slate-colored eyes rested for an instant on Estelle and then slid past her toward the Adam desk.

"It's about Ludwig," Estelle said. "I see no reason for not saying this. He deserves no consideration such as the rules of hospitality, and certainly no sympathy. You must understand that, Ann?"

"Yes, I do."

"I thought about Alice's death a good deal during the years while I lived in Paris and finally came to the conclusion that it was Ludwig who had killed her. Time and distance had given me a fresh perspective. During that dreadful period of the trial we were all too intense, too close to the tragedy to see things clearly. I told Justin it was Ludwig when I returned, and I feel I convinced him."

"But why, Estelle?"

"Because Ludwig was always so terribly careful of his health. The slightest scratch, and on went iodine. A touch of a cold or a sore throat, and he reeked of gargles. So many athletes and men with perfect physiques are that way. Don't you agree with me, Sergeant Hurlstone?"

"I do. Skip the perfect physique part and I'm that way myself."

"Well, one perfectly grim winter's day in Paris I suddenly thought how odd it was that Ludwig should have stayed out for so long a time that afternoon in the storm."

"I've also thought about that wet-clothes alibi," Ann said.

"My dear, when I remembered Ludwig's dread of colds, and the fact that he was supposed to have been out in that torrential downpour for over two hours, the entire thing became obvious. He hadn't been out at all. He simply *said* he was going out, but he never did go out until after he had killed Alice. Then he just ran out of doors for a minute or two and got soaking wet."

"Why would Ludwig have said a thing like that?"

"That he was going to go out into the storm? Sheer bravado. Ludwig started the word exhibitionism, I think. Everyone else was to be indoors all coddled and cozy while he was outside being rugged."

"Did he do that sort of thing to impress Alice?"

"Mostly so, yes. Also, it pleased him to show the other men up as weaklings. Especially when he had been drinking. Ludwig is pretty drastic, dear, when he drinks too much. I was rather worried this evening that he might have been starting in on one of his tears. Of course the other men always took it most good-naturedly, and that only spurred him on."

"How did Alice take it?"

"I thought about that in Paris too. I wondered whether Alice might have laughed."

"That's too farfetched, Estelle."

"It does seem so, doesn't it? But then you didn't know Ludwig."

"There is nothing farfetched about any motive," Sergeant Hurlstone said. "A woman on a farm south of here killed a neighbor over a mail-order teapot."

"But seriously, Estelle," Ann said, "you can't think that Ludwig killed Alice just because she laughed at him?"

"No, not directly, but a small spark can set off a vast explosion of dynamite. I do claim that a laugh from Alice could easily have been such a spark, and Ludwig had drunk so much both before and during luncheon that no one could tell how he would take things. You must remember that Ludwig was passionately in love with Alice, and I honestly believe that this love was a torture to him. You haven't seen the music room, have you?"

"No."

"Alice went there shortly after Ludwig had announced to all of us his intention of climbing South Knoll. As it came to me in Paris, I saw Ludwig coming into the music room wearing the same clothes he had worn at luncheon and their being bone dry. Even a raincoat couldn't have checked that torrent from sopping them. I saw many variations of the scene between Ludwig and Alice, torture and frustration and hopeless-ness on Ludwig's part, and Alice's helpless laughter. I saw her laughter change into outraged repudiation and scorn and all of Ludwig's hot emotions churning into an idiot rage. And at the end I always saw Ludwig seize the dagger from the case and kill Alice."

Estelle stood up. She said that this time she would disturb them no further. She said good night and left them quickly. She closed the door.

"What do you think of it?" Ann asked.

Sergeant Hurlstone remained standing. He placed the cat on the seat of the chair.

"I think it's good," he said, "so far as it goes. She forgot the key to the whole thing: the chow dog, Chin."

Sergeant Hurlstone left her. He toured the bedroom, dressing room, bathroom, and then came back.

"Drink tap water when you're thirsty," he said. "Go to bed now."

Ann took a parting look from the bedroom doorway. He had made a beeline for the Adam desk.

CHAPTER XXVI

It was a comfort to think of Sergeant Hurlstone so near by in the living room, sitting at Alice's desk, as she was now seated before Alice's dressing table. Ann felt she would sleep. A sound, healthy yawn overtook her.

Usually she read for a while after getting into bed, but tonight she did not do so. She turned out the bed lamp, and the room was momentarily sable until a luster from the clearing night sky sifted through it.

She lay with her eyes open in this shadowy darkness, too obsessed, after all, to sleep. What had it got her, this sudden transition from average unimportance into notoriety and vast wealth? She had always had enough money. She had had more than her share of happiness, and her worries had been very few.

Possibly this present wretched setup of violent, emotional wrenches and death, and the shadow of death, would be but a plunge through smashing surf into a quieter and less forceful sea. The swells would become smoother, and she could readjust herself. But to what?

What did she want? To become a career woman like Fanny? Ann thought not. No, women like Fanny had everything and nothing. They worked themselves pitilessly for some chimera which ever eluded them. They were in the center of life without ever being able to catch up with it. They had clothes and luxury and an endless celebrity, and some of them even had love. But they had no time to enjoy it.

Maybe there were no answers, Ann thought. Not only for Marlow heiresses but for anybody. Maybe only age was an answer. A full life and an exciting one, but get it out of your system early. Maybe then you could be at peace and happy.

If you had a family.

If you had Bill.

Quite suddenly in this tremulous darkness she made up her mind what to do about Bill. She felt inspiration in it, and a deep sense of gratitude. Clarence Harlan could help her. It was not too late to ask him now. He, too, would just have retired.

She reached for the phone on the bed table and took it from its cradle. She asked to be connected with Harlan.

"This is Ann," she said to him, "and I'm sorry about the hour."

"It's a splendid hour. What can I do?"

"It's about Bill."

"Planning your campaign?"

"Yes. You said that you had looked up his family?"

"Practically back to the Pharaohs. Not a pirate in it. No horse thieves. Nobody hanged. The dullest bunch of sterling characters I ever heard of in my life."

"I don't want a horse thief. I want military men. Surely they went to the wars?"

"If my splendid memory serves me, and it better had, they did. Which war do you want?"

"All of them, please."

Harlan gave them not alone with detail but with added details, especially on the distaff side, which Ann occasionally requested. Then she thanked him with a warmth which all but reached Harlan across the wire and said good night.

She closed her eyes.

She slept.

The room had a pallid tinge when she woke up. Around four or five o'clock it would be, or thereabouts. Ann was tremendously refreshed. How quiet things were. She put on a wrapper and opened the living-room door.

Sergeant Hurlstone was not there. Nor was the cat. What was that cat act anyhow? It had seemed out of character, completely so, and had been so pointedly prolonged. Surely a pat and a "nice pussy" would have been enough without that tender lugging of the beast all over the house.

The sergeant had left a light burning by the Adam desk, focused on a sheet of note paper propped against an inkwell. His handwriting was strong and precisely legible:

> I have certain immediate things to do *[the note read]* and am hampered by a lack of assistants or having anyone whom I can trust to stay with you. I will not wake you, as you will need plenty of strength to get through the day. I will lock the door from the outside and shove the key back under the sill. I shall not be long. Stay here until I return.
>
> James Hurlstone, Sgt.
> 5:27 A.M.

It was later than Ann had thought. She looked at her watch: twenty minutes to six. Sergeant Hurlstone had been gone, then, for a quarter of an hour. She picked up the key from the base of the door and put it back in the lock.

The fire in the grate had died. The daylight was a dismal gray, and Ann went to a window and looked out into a veil of mist which blurred the nearest trees. An intense gloom came over her and the recurrence of an irritating sense of dread. She felt the need of the armament of clothes, swiftly to dress and be prepared against this nervous imminence of something to come.

She was finishing her hair when the house phone rang. Surely, Ann thought, it would be Sergeant Hurlstone, calm with some fresh-hewn horror. But Washburn's voice said when she answered it: "I regret troubling you at this early hour, Miss Marlow."

"What is it, Washburn?"

"The airfield reports that a plane has just made a crash landing. Neither the pilot nor Mr. William Forrest were hurt, and Mr. Forrest insists upon being driven to the house and upon seeing you immediately. The situation is a little unusual, as Mr. Forrest is in the service of the United States Marine Corps and has made several startling statements as to results if his wishes are not complied with. It is all so confusing and irregular that I have taken the liberty of disturbing you."

Ann instantly felt like champagne: swiftly glittering and aglow.

"What wagons are there, Washburn?"

"I beg pardon?"

"What kinds?"

"Oh, I see. There are the victoria that met you, a landaulet, a surrey, and a barouche."

"Is the barouche lined with plush?"

"Why—yes, I believe it is."

"Then send it for Mr. Forrest, please."

"I will give instructions immediately."

"Thank you, and I'll be in the lounge."

CHAPTER XXVII

Everything was driven from Ann's head but the thought of seeing Bill. Certainly her wits were. She concentrated exclusively on just how much he meant to her and how meaningless any existence would be without him.

Furthermore, she had him cold.

She was glad that her hair was done, as she wanted to hurry down and take possession of the arena before the lamb stepped into it. After a moment's intensive indecision she chose and put on a dress of white organdy. It was one she had gone overboard about at a recent sale: a time-bomb trinket which exploded in your face just as you were lulled by its sweet simplicity, a simplicity which artfully revived the dated ravishments of the twenties.

Ann unlocked the living-room door and went out into the hall, which was pallid with a light misting softly in through its mullioned windows. Her head was still witless of everything but Bill, and she forgot the lift and started walking down broad marble stairs carpeted in taupe.

The flight went no farther than the floor below, and in front of her stretched a companion to the hallway above. She saw at its farther end the ornate head of another stairway.

This hallway was also pierced with mullioned windows, the misted light from which gave an almost ethereal effect to its occasional pieces of furniture and to dark canvases of the Flemish school which were on its walls.

Ann had already taken several steps before a wit revived and advised her abruptly that this was the second floor.

The music room was on this floor.

This was the floor on which Alice had been killed.

A swift urge pressed Ann to run, to run swiftly through the hall's unearthly twilight to the safety of the stairhead at its distant end. She controlled this impulse and walked on, stepping softly, conscious of her stepping.

Halfway along it she came to an open doorway on her left, flanked by two deep alcoves. The beauty of a great salon compelled her to stop on the threshold, to look in.

That would be the spinet over there. Those were the cases. What was it Harlan had said? Rare coins, some excellent folios, some weapons. One of which had been the Cellini dagger which the murderer, in his flush of red mania, had seized and plunged deep into that pitiable sheath. At one end of the vast salon was the console of a great organ. Tall windows were portiered in peach damask. Pale silk paneled the walls.

Alice: the tragic stranger who had been her mother.

A rush of sympathy for this murdered stranger swamped Ann and suddenly brought her to tears. A love welled up no less strong because it was so late. A grief that strengthened the tears and blinded her. She went to the spinet and touched the keys which her mother had touched. She knew that she was being maudlin, but she did not care.

"Alice."

So strongly was the spirit of Alice in her that for an instant Ann felt no shock at hearing the spoken name. She turned slowly and faced Ludwig, who had walked up softly close to her. Ludwig's bold features were flushed, and his dark, prominent eyes held a light of wild incredulity.

This is the way a man looks, it occurred to Ann, when he has seen a ghost. He thinks me Alice or her spirit because of this dress, this misted light, my resemblance to my mother. She must then have looked as I look now.

An hypnosis of clamping terror held her. Urgently she wanted to scream into Ludwig's boldly carved face across the deep flush of which was spreading a heavy dewing of clammy sweat. Urgently she wished to run.

"Alice, my love."

Ludwig came closer, and his breath was sodden with liquor. He still wore his dinner clothes, and the shirt was sweated and stained with spilled drink. There was an overpowering physical force about Ludwig right then. Ann felt it in his thick arms and barrel chest, in the hair-covered fingers that were curved rigid with astonishment and shock.

(*Ludwig is pretty drastic, dear, when he drinks too much*, Estelle had said just so recently to her and to Sergeant Hurlstone. *No one could tell how he would take things.*)

Ann's own stupor lessened, and she managed to say with reasonable lucidity: "It's this dress I have on, Ludwig. I'm Ann. Alice is dead."

He observed her shrewdly with drunken disbelief, suspicious of some trick. The fumes increased and receded with sickening waves through his head.

"What are you doing here, then?" he said.

"I stopped on my way down to the lounge."

"At this time in the morning?"

"A friend of mine just got here by plane. Bill Forrest."

"You're lying."

"Let me by, please, Ludwig."

"No."

She wished to heaven that she could stop trembling, could even control her chattering teeth. A scream would be the worst thing she could go in for, although she felt desperately like loosing one. The chances were one in a thousand that anyone would hear it. Certainly no one could act on it in time. Those fingers were still tensed. Ludwig would simply be inflamed by the shriek and would choke her.

"What do you want, then, Ludwig?"

"I want to know what you are doing here."

"I've told you."

"Don't toy with me. I've been up all night. I'm drunk. I'm in no mood for silly lies. You all think I'm a murderer. I'm not. I'm a truthful, unhappy, miserable man. Every time I've come to this house I've spent hours during the night in this room."

Ludwig's voice grew increasingly thick. It was hard to understand him. He spewed out the thoughts as randomly as they reeked through his head.

"There is something hidden in this room. I've never been able to find it. The murderer wants it. All last night I sat in that alcove in the corridor and watched. I heard the murderer come in here just a moment before you came in here. He didn't come out again, so he is in here now with us. But we can't see him."

"There is no one here, Ludwig. Just you and me." Ludwig wrestled with this for a while. His bloodshot eyes roved heavily about the great salon. He weaved slowly on his feet, impatient for combat with this killer who was now so miraculously endowed with a power of invisibility. His fingers remained rigidly curved.

"You have let him go."

"No, Ludwig."

"The white back. Alice." Ludwig's face went to pieces. He grimaced horribly, and his color grew apoplectic. "*You* are Alice."

He stifled her denial by crushing her close to his barrel chest. He forced her face up and smothered it with kisses. He muttered brokenly: "I've been waiting for this, darling. For years I've been waiting."

Rage and nausea carried her fingers raking across his cheek. The pain bewildered Ludwig, and for a moment he stood holding her and looking at her stupidly. He reached a hand up and brushed some blood from his cheek. He looked affronted and hurt.

He said petulantly, "You've scarred me."

Fumes swept through him, and he threw her roughly against the spinet. Ann struck its keyboard and fell to the floor.

Ludwig turned and walked steadily out of the room. He closed the door.

Six-ten a.m.

CHAPTER XXVIII

SIX-TEN A.M.

The pilot viewed the landing gear with disgust.

"You go ahead," he said. "I'll stick around while they do a job on this."

Bill followed the coachman's strapping back. He took in the perfection of a whipcord uniform, the boots, the hat, the cockade. He took in the barouche. The folding top over the back seat was down. Plush purred and varnish gleamed. A mare was superb in chestnut satin.

Bill stepped in.

I will now, he thought, be bewitched into Bette Davis starring as the Belle of Old Chickamauga, Tennessee.

He sat down.

The coachman mounted the driver's seat.

The mare extended herself slenderly into a Currier and Ives.

The barouche rolled.

CHAPTER XXIX

SIX-TEN A.M.

"Is there no service around here?" Ludwig asked the lounge at large.

Ludwig held his finger (having found it) pressed on the bell button. He was, he knew, very drunk. And he was bad. Pity about giving Ann that push. Not gentlemanly. But what did that matter nowadays? Chivalry was a drug on the market. Too many women in pants. Impossible to exercise punctilio to a pair of pants. Somebody would take care of her. Because somebody had gone into the music room just before she had. A sprite, no less, who believed in hide-and-seek.

He wanted to cry. Nobody liked him. *Really* cared for him in the sense of fussing tenderly over him when he was hurt. The scratches on his cheek were beginning to smart. Let the she-devil lie by her spinet. Let her dance a farandola with the sprite. He wanted iodine. He wanted a drink. He wanted lots of things.

"You rang, Mr. Appleby?"

"I think I did."

Washburn eyed Ludwig's hair-covered forefinger.

"I believe you are still ringing, sir."

"Well, so I am. I want a lot of things."

"Yes?"

"I want iodine; I want a decanter of scotch, and I want Mr. Harlan."

"Very good, sir."

"Telephone for Mr. Harlan first. Wake him up. Get him down here."

Washburn, expensively impervious, went to the house telephone.

"Well?" Ludwig said.

"I am ringing his rooms, Mr. Appleby."

"Carry on."

A moment passed.

Ludwig, in slow motion, moved to the sofa and sat down.

"Well?" Ludwig said.

"Mr. Harlan does not answer."

"Ring again."

The sofa was Knoll, softly cushioned in lime damask over goose down. Ludwig nested pillows. All else had failed, Ludwig decided, but at least this sofa loved him. How tenderly it enfolded.

"What in the devil is the matter with him?" he asked. "There is still no answer, sir."

"Try once more."

Ludwig's desire to see Harlan was alcoholically vague.

Somewhere there was a purpose in it. A monetary one. Justin was dead, and he had just pushed Ann into a spinet. Would she skip it and let the bygone push be bygone? No. Estelle was no good. Estelle hated him. Anyhow, she thought he was the murderer and was out to see him hanged. Well, something might be done with Harlan. Money.

"I'm sorry, sir, but Mr. Harlan does not answer. Shall I go up and see?"

"Yes, but bring me the iodine first, and the scotch and ice and a siphon."

"Certainly, sir."

Washburn started for the service door.

"And," Ludwig said, "a glass."

CHAPTER XXX

SIX-TEN A.M.

The laboratory at Black Tor was located in a separate building removed at about a five minutes' walk from the house.

It was a large room, a vast one almost, and it had been as expensively equipped by Dr. Johnson (with Marlow's money) as that of any in the country. Even the cinematic settings for Mrs. Shelley's young student of physiology, Frankenstein, scarcely offered laboratories more cluttered in glittering devices and in chemical scope.

Under a shaft of white light on a gleaming white table top lay the dark-haired cat. It was frankly bored. It yawned as insultingly as possible and stretched black satin legs. It sent a lethal look upward into the shaft of white light.

Medical Examiner Bedmann looked at Sergeant Hurlstone with bewilderment.

"I don't know what you dragged me out of bed for," he said. "There is nothing the matter with this cat at all."

Sergeant Hurlstone remained granite.

"Have you made every test that you can, Doctor?"

"For the set of premises which you outlined, yes."

"Will you need notes on them?"

"No. What for?"

"You will be asked to testify in detail concerning them at the trial. Also concerning Miss Ann Marlow's carafe of drinking water. When I brought the carafe down here last night you and Dr. Johnson were completing the autopsy of Mr. Marlow. The cadaver was on that table over in that corner of the room. Is that right?"

"Certainly it is."

"Try not to be impatient with me, Doctor. I am trying to impress these things firmly on your memory."

"I'm not impatient. I just don't get it."

"You will. I put the carafe down on that small table over there in the center of that wall. I requested that neither of you touch it, to preserve fingerprints, but that whatever water you required for your test for poison be drawn out by a syringe. This all comes back to you?"

"Yes."

"Dr. Johnson then assembled the equipment and chemicals necessary for testing for various poisons while you were continuing with the autopsy and I was explaining to you the circumstances surrounding Miss Ann Marlow's suspicions. You will recall that I spoke of the metallic click, Miss Estelle Marlow's entering the dressing room, and Miss Ann Marlow's subsequent observing that the drinking glass had just been used."

"What are you leading up to, Sergeant?"

"Shortly, Doctor. Now the materials required to test for pyrogallol were already on hand, as both you and Dr. Johnson had by then agreed on pyrogallol being in all probability the immediate cause of Mr. Marlow's death. I am right so far?"

"You are."

"You then left your work on the cadaver and tested the water in the carafe."

"I did, and it contained enough pyrogallol to make a swallow of it fatal. What put it into your head that this cat had been given some too?"

"The fact that before I brought the carafe down here I had forced the cat to swallow what would amount to about two ordinary swallows of the water."

"Then it should have been a dead cat about six hours ago.

"It isn't."

Dr. Bedmann was profoundly shocked.

"Was the carafe always with you until you brought it down here, Sergeant? Could no one have had access to it?"

"It was with me from the moment when I took it from Miss Ann Marlow's bed table. The water was pure, Doctor, *up to the moment when I left the carafe on that table over there.*"

"Of course. Otherwise the cat would be dead. This is dumfounding, and I can make no sense in it. Why on earth would Dr. Johnson deliberately introduce a solution of pyrogallol into a carafe of perfectly pure water? I certainly didn't. You didn't. Nobody else was in here but Johnson."

"Yes, Dr. Johnson did it. The pyrogallol solution was already at hand. He had used some of it earlier in the day to kill Marlow. Remember, he had just overheard me telling you Miss Ann Marlow's suspicions about the carafe. He knew that if the water were found to contain poison Miss Estelle Marlow would almost certainly be accused."

"Quick thinking, that."

"Dr. Johnson's thoughts have had considerable practice along such lines. It seemed a heaven-sent opportunity to stamp Miss Estelle Marlow as Suspect Number One for Justin Marlow's murder. So he poured the pyrogallol into the carafe while you and I were standing talking beside the cadaver. He was completely certain it would be taken for granted that the pyrogallol had been introduced during the time when the carafe had been upstairs in Miss Ann Marlow's bedroom. He was assured of this because *he did not know* that I had already started an immediate test by forcing this cat to take some of the water after the carafe was in my possession. It is the act that will convict him."

"Of Marlow? Of that earlier one?"

"That's right. All of them."

"Aren't you taking a chance by accusing him on the basis of that carafe business alone?"

"I'm not. There's more than that. A chow dog called Chin. An Adam desk. A mess back in Boston. Care to come with me?"

"Where?"

"To arrest him."

Six-fourteen a.m.

CHAPTER XXXI

SIX-FOURTEEN A.M.

Bill stepped from the barouche.

He was beginning to feel foolish, not from the barouche, but because he had come to Black Tor at all. That butler's voice over the telephone hadn't sounded as though Ann were in dire peril, and the coachman hadn't resembled any minion from a Fu Manchu's lair. Neither had the horse.

What had Ann meant by that "widower" crack with its vivid trimmings about pyrogallol and about the next time their cooking up something fresh? Then hanging up.

All right. He was a dupe. Lured here by her wiles and craft. Coldly formal would be the word for it. No, I must have misunderstood you, Ann, my dear. Sorry. Bad connection, wasn't it? And Freska's is always so noisy. Never a moment without its hurtling bottle and planted mouse. I just came up because I wanted to say good-by to you anyhow. Before going. No, better not add an Over There. Just keep it dignified, restrained, and simple.

Possibly he would let himself be persuaded to breakfast (he was hungry as the dickens), but all on a socially formal plane. An English breakfast, Bill decided, from the looks of the dive. Several yards of crested silver warming dishes. Eggs, kidneys, sausages, hashed brown potatoes, collops, and English brawn.

Bill was glad to see that Washburn looked like his voice. Bill gave him his service cap. He followed Washburn for a half day's march to the lounge.

"Miss Marlow said she would receive you in here, Mr. Forrest."

"Thank you."

Washburn bowed, vanished.

Bill walked into the lounge. He spotted Ludwig just about the moment when Ludwig spotted him. Ludwig was enchanted. He studied Bill's uniform.

"There's no use in shooting," he said. "I haven't a patch of white left in my eyes. I'm Ludwig Appleby. Who are you?"

"Bill Forrest."

"That's right. Ann said you were dropping in. I didn't believe her. Have a drink, Mr. Forrest?"

"Thank you, I will."

"I'll try to get my hand loose from the decanter. It's stuck. I'm drunk."

"Sound idea."

"I thought so. There. Help yourself."

Bill helped himself.

"How is Miss Marlow, Mr. Appleby?"

"Ann? Fine, fine. She is dancing a farandola with a sprite."

"Good for her. Was she up all night too?"

"No, just me. I sat out in the hall waiting for a murderer." Ludwig stared unbelievably at the apparition of a Washburn coming toward them on a run. "Look! He's running."

Washburn, extremely pale and out of breath, stopped short by the sofa.

"Gentlemen, Sergeant Hurlstone has just telephoned from Dr. Johnson's house. He wishes Miss Ann Marlow located immediately. She failed to answer the telephone in her rooms. I beg you to believe how serious this is. Dr. Johnson is not at home, and Sergeant Hurlstone is afraid the doctor's purpose is to do Miss Marlow some bodily harm. Sergeant Hurlstone is on his way here now." Washburn caught up with his breath and blurted it out: "Dr. Johnson is the murderer. En masse."

Bill looked at Ludwig's glazing eyes. He didn't like them.

"Appleby!" he said sharply. "You know where she is. What did you mean about dancing a farandola and that sprite stuff?"

"About what, Mr. Forrest?"

"Where is Ann?"

Ludwig waved Bill away with a petulant gesture. "Did you say Johnson, Washburn?"

"Yes."

"Johnson is the murderer?"

"Yes."

"Poor Ann."

The excitement was too much.

Ludwig passed out.

CHAPTER XXXII

SIX-FOURTEEN A.M.

Dr. Johnson sat tense and cramped in the darkness.

The metal pipes of the 16 double open diapason of the great organ towered above him through dusty murk. The small panel door through which he had come from the music room was tightly closed.

Ann Marlow, he knew, had followed him into the music room, but her attention had immediately been held by the spinet, which had given him time to slip through the little doorway. There had been voices, muffled, unclear, but the man's voice had sounded like Ludwig's.

Then silence.

They were gone, probably, but Dr. Johnson thought it safer to wait for a while. His legs were annoyed because of their cramped position, and he was annoyed because his being shoved in there among the organ pipes wasn't dignified. Funny how in later years dignity had come to mean so much.

Funny, too, how year after year for twenty long years he should have kept searching for that damned letter and never have found it.

How strongly Ann had resembled Alice when she had come into the music room just now. So much more so than she had on the day before. Possibly the white dress with the hint in its cut of an earlier day had done the trick.

Really, she had looked almost exactly as Alice had looked when Alice had confronted him about the contents of the letter. Alice had not been wearing white, it was true, but the cut of her gown had been the same.

He could understand—he had always been able to understand—why his mother had written that letter to Alice.

His mother and father had both been of stern Puritan stock, and he had always known that his father's fatal stroke had been brought on by the discovery of his affair with Janette Maynew and his illegal operation which had resulted in Janette's death.

Then had come his mother's immediate attack of brain fever, brought on by the death of his father, with her writing to Alice during her single moment of lucidity just before she died.

His mother had had to write that letter.

She would have considered it a moral duty she could never have evaded even though it meant the ruin of her son. Alice's family, the Charings, had always been their charges, and Alice was to have a child and trusted him. So his mother would have reasoned it out.

He remembered some of the phrases Alice had quoted from his mother's letter: "unworthy of a place in that honored and splendid profession to which his father and his grandfather had dedicated their lives." That had been one of them.

It was while she had been quoting this phrase that Alice had been standing with her back close to the grill-work masking the sesquialtera of the great organ, and her hands had been behind her, holding something. He had thought it at the time to be a handkerchief, but it could have been the letter, which was why he had always considered the music room as the best place to search for it. Then again, when she had walked over to the spinet, he had thought there had been nothing in her hands.

Always he believed that this going of Alice's to the spinet had been the move which had set off the fatal ending. It was her "dismissal" of him, done in the fashion of the lady of the period. Even now he flushed in remembrance of his pleading that she reconsider her intention (her duty, she had called it) to expose him. An exposure which certainly would have thrown him out of his profession and exposed him to a murder charge for the illegal operation which had resulted in Janette's death.

Pleading? Never would he permit the knowledge to come out of its hiding place in his secret mind that he had groveled, literally, at her feet.

Then his love—for he *had* loved her a little, as much so as he had been capable of loving anyone other than himself—even that tepid thing had been taken out and spread before her.

And her words: "Go, please. Don't let me add disgust to my pity for you."

She had spoken the words over her shoulder, not even turning to say them to him (actually she could not stand his transformation into such abjectness, but he had taken the whole spinet performance as the curt dismissal of a servant, whereas in reality Alice had not had the heart to look at him), so his head had suddenly filled with fire and he had killed her.

Even as he had walked from the room (so quickly had his *amour-propre* started working to excuse him) that thing from Wilde had come into his head as a palliative sop to mitigate the horrendous nature of his deed: "For all men kill the thing they love."

How could he explain such things, such imponderables, at a trial? Should he ever be brought to trial, which he felt certain he would not. Well, he wouldn't bother. He felt very safe, still in his private nirvana which was of his own creation, which had grown each year stronger as the years so securely had come and gone.

He hadn't found the letter, so nobody would.

Alice (he had sometimes thought this) could well have destroyed it before summoning him to the music room to denounce him. She had issued this summons over the house telephone, thank God, so no one but he and she had known of it.

Certainly the letter had not been in the drawer of her desk, where she kept her private correspondence. He had gone up and looked for it there right after killing her.

That was when Frank Lawrence had caught a glimpse of him just as he left Alice's room, but in the immediate excitement the fact had not registered with Frank as being of any importance. Dr. Johnson had then run to his own rooms (he was staying in the house then and did not have a house of his own on the grounds as he had now) and hurriedly taken off his white surgeon's smock because it was bloodstained. He had worn the smock in the first place as a harmless jest, because he had thought that Alice's telephoned summons was simply for him to take another look at the injured foot of her chow, Chin.

He had put on the dark tweed coat which went with his trousers and later he had destroyed the bloodstained smock. But the remembrance of Lawrence's glimpse of him wearing it continued to worry him. A stupid fellow, Lawrence, but even so the thought had preyed upon Dr. Johnson so after a while he had doctored the *pâté* of *foie gras* with ptomaine and had got Lawrence out of the way.

A clever man could deduce most of this—say a man like Sergeant Hurlstone, if he once got on the track. Certainly, if through some amazing and cruel chance or purpose he ever got hold of the letter, then a mind like Sergeant Hurlstone's easily would fit everything into its proper place.

The silence remained unbroken.

Surely he had waited long enough.

He stood up and tentatively started to open the little door. He heard no sound. He opened the door wide and stepped out into the music room.

Then he turned and carefully shut the little door.

CHAPTER XXXIII

SIX-EIGHTEEN A.M.

Dr. Johnson could not determine what Ann was doing there.

She was seated on the floor with her back resting against the spinet. One ankle was in her hand, as though she had been rubbing it. He thought she must have fainted and have just come to. Her eyes were startlingly wide open as they stared at him in fright. Yes, surely it was fright. He smiled at her reassuringly.

Then he stopped smiling because what could he say? Scarcely that he had just stepped in to examine the 16 double open diapason. A devil of a mess, now that he thought of it. He didn't want to kill her. Queer that in spite of all the others he revolted at the thought of killing Ann. Possibly it was because he had given her life, because he had brought breath to her even though Alice had been dead.

Yes, that would be it. But he'd have to do something about his appearing so oddly like this. Possibly, quite possibly, she would not know about the structural features of great organs. The little door might signify nothing to her beyond a door to another room or a hallway. "What happened, Miss Marlow?"

"I'm quite all right, Doctor."

"Let me help you."

Her voice stopped him.

"No—please—"

Ann stood up swiftly and faced him, with her back pressed against the keyboard, her fingers gripping its ivory keys. Her lips winced once, and he wondered again about her ankle.

"I take the liberty of coming in here, sometimes very early in the morning. I have a modest talent for the spinet. I find pleasure in exercising it."

"Yes, Doctor."

"You're trembling."

"No—really, I'm perfectly all right."

Ann did not know about the structure of the great organ, and so the spinet-playing excuse for Dr. Johnson's being there held a reasonable note. And Ludwig, after all, had been very drunk. But this did not hold water. There was something about Dr. Johnson's manner—stupid to call it an emanation, but that was what it amounted to—queer, and furtively evil, and deadly. It seeped through his pleasant surface like a miasma. But no *doctor* would—doctor—men in white—white—"Doctor, do you ever wear those—smocks, do you call them? You see them on surgeons in the movies."

Dr. Johnson's smile froze.

"Very rarely, Miss Marlow."

"But you have worn them?"

"Why?"

Fool! He knew why. He knew that Ann suppressed a scream. Of course she had been brighter than all the rest of them about Ludwig's all-but-forgotten riddle of the white back in the window: one that was not a shirt, or a dress, or a coat. Jerry Abbott had been bright about it, too, so he had had to arrange the "hunting accident" to kill Jerry Abbott, for Abbott had found him in the laboratory one morning and had laughingly suggested that "there was Ludwig's white back." He had never worn another one after that.

Ludwig with his riddle still lived on unmurdered because Dr. Johnson preferred him to. Ludwig not only offered a good suspect for Estelle to hint at, but it had been to Ludwig's financial advantage that the riddle remain unsolved, even should the smock idea have crossed his mind. Anyhow, he could always take care of Ludwig should he have to. Something along the line of induced apoplexy would turn the trick.

Well, it was too bad about Ann. He would have to kill her now that she had solved the white-back riddle. How stupid of her. How wretchedly *stupid* of her to have thought it up. And how unkind to him.

But perhaps it would be for the best. She probably had a whole lot of Justin Marlow's tenacity in her. She would keep on the trail as doggedly as Justin had.

He had hoped that with Justin out of the way the whole thing would die from inanition. The radioactive substance given to Justin years ago when Justin had started in so actively to clear Fred's name had seemed such a foolproof answer and so secure.

Estelle certainly would never have bothered to pursue the quest, and who else was there? No one, until Justin had produced Ann so swiftly out of a hat. That was why the pyrogallol had been used to speed the more leisurely radium: Ann's appearance and the fact that she had been put in Alice's rooms which were, in consequence, opened for the first time since Alice's death.

How confusing such webs were when you became enmeshed in them! You scarcely knew where to turn or why. The point eventually was reached where your brain refused to function any longer with clarity. Why *had* the opening up of Alice's rooms panicked him so? Was it again the letter? He had never had access to them after that moment when he had looked through her desk just after having killed her. Or had it been that wretched bad luck of Ann's taking the ocelots with the grim result of the skeleton bones in silver on the films?

Now *there* (Dr. Johnson's busy brain grew once more pleasantly clear and sharp) he had been amazingly clever in having taken that bull by its horns, for the enlargements were bound to become a nine days' wonder, and any physician would have recognized the bone patterns for what they were, any layman, even, who had ever seen an X-ray shot.

Yes, kill her and get it over with, and that would be the last.

"Why are you up so early, Miss Marlow?"

"A friend has just landed at the airfield, Doctor."

No, choking her would never do. Not if Estelle were to be suspected of it, the pyrogallol-in-the-carafe attempt of Estelle's having presumably failed. That bit of inspirational chicanery still stood up nicely in its use to pin Justin's murder on Estelle.But how simple! The case of antique weapons was still at hand, just as it had been at hand when he had lolled Alice. Not the Cellini dagger, of course. He smiled faintly. Justin had disposed of that. But there were others. His eyes darted slyly toward the case and considered a thin stiletto of Spanish steel. Just such a weapon as Estelle might choose.

"Were you on your way downstairs to meet your friend, Miss Marlow?"

"Yes, Doctor."

He moved several casual steps and reached the case. He wished Ann would do something. An overt cue to force him into the distasteful plunge. He *wanted* her to scream now, because then one hand could press the scream back while his other hand took the stiletto from the case. Or if she would run. Anything but this detestable standing there and staring at him, shaking with terror. It was fear hypnosis that held her, he supposed. For an instant he examined her clinically. Yes, that was it.

Mother, Ann thought, was right here too. Only her back was toward him on that distant afternoon, and she didn't know he was going to kill her. She never saw him take the dagger from the case, as Ann was seeing him. Mother—Mother—*darling Mother, what shall I do?*

He had the stiletto in his hand, having lifted it as though he were just casually examining it. How chill the grip felt, just as had the Cellini one. Ail right. Get it over with.

He was prepared for her screaming or for her making a break toward the door. He was prepared even for her coming out of her hypnosis and attacking him. He was prepared against anything but what she did do: her sagging to the floor and her saying: "My ankle is sprained. I am in pain. Would you help me, Doctor?" She said again: "Doctor—"

His loose lips quivered, and for a brief instant all the torture of his lifetime seemed to strike him. Then he smiled down at her pityingly. Silly little fool! Practically hurling the Hippocratic oath in his teeth, as if for years that tear-jerking rubbish any longer had had the power to affect him. But her sagging down at his feet had confused him, just as this sudden clattering of many other feet behind him was confusing him. He raised the stiletto to strike.

And so they found him.

CHAPTER XXXIV

The four-part Sheraton table was still reduced to a conversational size, and Estelle, in her seating, had thrown Mrs. Post to the winds.

Sergeant Hurlstone and Bill flanked her. She wanted to chip from Sergeant Hurlstone the steps that had led him to his astonishing solution of the case. Estelle shuddered when she considered what Dr. Johnson might have done to her sinus—like that mad doctor who had upset Paris ten years ago through his glittering habit of inserting typhoid virus into occasional pills.

And she wanted to size up Bill.

Ann found herself between Sergeant Hurlstone and Clarence Harlan, whose early rising and absence from his rooms when Washburn had rung had been due to Estelle. Estelle also had wakened early in a dread of worry over her situation as Chief Suspect and had summoned Harlan to talk things over.

Medical Examiner Bedmann was not present because he was taking care of Dr. Johnson, after Dr. Johnson had broken down and completely gone to pieces.

Ludwig was not present because Bill had landed a haymaker and broken Ludwig's nose.

It was the least, Bill had felt, he could do. After he finished breakfast and said good-by and was gone, then, of course, if Ludwig again pushed Ann into a spinet somebody else would have to take care of re-breaking Ludwig's nose.

Sad, Bill thought, helping himself largely to broiled kidneys and bacon, that it should all end like this. Tough on everybody. Tough on Marlow, who had led such a rottenly unhappy life, only to be murdered at the end of it. Alice and Fred, Ann's parents—a rotten business that was for your money. Tough on himself too.

Bill decided he would never marry at all, now that Ann with her millions was definitely out. Maybe the war would take care of it and save him, via a bachelor's grave, from a celibatic old age.

Bill listened absently while Sergeant Hurlstone said to Estelle: "Most desks of the Adam period had secret compartments in them. Wall safes were unheard of in that day, and people wanted some reasonably secure place for their private papers. I knew that Alice Marlow had used the desk constantly for writing her poetry, and it was perfectly probable that she should have come upon the secret compartment in time. It was the sort of romantic thing she would have wanted to keep to herself, even from her husband, and of course she would have put the letter from Dr. Johnson's mother in it."

"But what made you interested in the desk in the first place?"

"Motive. For twenty years everyone had more or less taken it for granted that Alice Marlow's murder was a crime of passion, that jealousy had been at the base of it, or love. Every one of Mr. Marlow's investigations had concentrated along that line and they had come to nothing. So it probably was something else. That left the rest of the string. Blackmail, threats, fear—things usually based on a paper or a document of some kind. Well—"

Bill, with no hesitation, accepted more kidneys from Washburn. He let Sergeant Hurlstone rattle on, giving him even less than half an ear, until he heard Ann say: "What was the point you made so much of about the chow dog, Chin?"

"The dog's just lying there and trembling while her mistress was being stabbed was the point. That meant that Mrs. Marlow's attacker was either somebody the dog had absolute confidence in, or else it meant a person whom even a chow would be afraid of. Now Danning, your maid, had told us in her testimony that Chin had cut her foot on the morning of the crime and that Dr. Johnson had treated it and bandaged it up. Probably Dr. Johnson had given the dog a lot of care."

"Of course. Chin trusted him."

"Perhaps, but in any case Dr. Johnson would fit in either as someone in whom the dog had confidence or of whom she was afraid. As a matter of fact, the whole outline of the case pointed to the murderer having more than an average knowledge of medical matters and drugs. Take the ptomaine, the radioactive substance, the effects of pyrogallol, especially when pyrogallol fitted so aptly as an additional irritant to Mr. Marlow's disease—all of those things cried Doctor quite obviously, and in this business when you settle on the obvious you usually find that—"

On and on and on, Bill felt, will he go. Normally Bill would have been avidly interested. Not now. His hunger sated, the gnawing ache had moved back from his stomach to his heart. How lovely she was. How lovely she always had been. How sad.

Washburn, at this point, announced the press.

The landing field, Washburn intimated, was black with planes which were at the instant disgorging reporters, cameramen, sob sisters, and apparati for the newsreel men.

Clarence Harlan at once took command.

He said to Ann: "Just leave them to me. In my long, long day I have eaten more reporters than that young man of yours has just eaten kidneys."

"I am not her young man," Bill said coldly.

"That is what you think, Mr. Forrest. Washburn, please herd the mass of them into the lounge. Break out gallons of your finest whiskies. Prepare steaming pots of coffee—sandwiches, toast, eggs. There will be no need for you to resort to forcible feeding. Ann, do not worry. By the time Washburn gets through with them they'll barely want to interview me, much less you."

"But I want them to interview me."

"What?"

"I want to give them an interview right now."

"My dear child, you don't realize what you're saying."

"I realize perfectly, and I have not been bereft of my senses. I suppose they'll cover most of the papers in the country?"

"Nothing so modest as a country."

"Good! Washburn, please let me know the minute they're in the corral."

CHAPTER XXXV

Photofloods flooded; cranks ground, and Graflexes synchronized with flash bulbs.

The worst, the really bad part of it, was over. Ann had frankly and with sincerity expressed her feelings regarding her change from being a Ledrick into becoming a Marlow. She had touched on her genuine sorrow and shock at Marlow's death.

She saw that Harlan had stopped looking at her with anguished worry and that he was regarding her with a rather awed admiration. Bill's face wasn't bad either, although he did look puzzled.

"This may strike you as a breach of taste, gentlemen," Ann said, "but you and your readers will understand the situation in which I find myself. For some time before Mr. Marlow's tragic death, before either of us had the faintest inkling of my relationship to the Marlows, I had accepted Private William Forrest's proposal of marriage." Lenses veered; bulbs flashed; Bill's mouth opened, and it stayed open until it occurred to him to close it. The pictures of this (next day) enchanted Fanny. She cut out as many as she could find of them and varnished them to the inside of an aquarium as a goal for the fish to aim at.

"Mr. Forrest has just enlisted in the Marines. Ordinarily Mr. Marlow's death would have deferred our marriage for a suitable length of time, but Mr. Forrest is going away. As I have said, you will understand and your readers will understand. That is why I am announcing the engagement now."

She gauged the flush of rage mounting on Bill's cheeks. "Mr. Forrest," Ann hurried on, "is making the Army his career. It is his hope and my hope that in the years to come he may rise to the rank of his great-grandfather, General Lawrence Montague Forrest, whose—"

"How in—? How do you know anything about—?"

"Never mind! General Lawrence Montague Forrest, whose record was so splendid during the Civil War. I am sure you will understand when I add that General Forrest's wife was Virginia Abigail Braddock, of the Washington Braddocks, a family of great wealth. If Mr. Forrest had intended to continue in civilian life the difference in our financial standings would have been embarrassing, but with a military career before him no such embarrassment could possibly exist, especially with the precedent for such a match already established in his family."

Ann thought she heard Harlan mutter: "I ought to take her into my firm." She noticed that Bill's face had lost its fiery look and seemed dazed.

She heard a reporter asking whether there were any definite plans as yet for the wedding.

"There are," Ann said. "Mr. Forrest will have left for service by the end of the week. We will be married on Friday by a justice of the peace. It was Friday you had decided upon, wasn't it, Bill?"

"Yes. And as soon as this interview is ended I'm going to fix up a date for you with Ludwig and a spinet."

ABOUT RUFUS KING

Rufus King (1893–1966) was an American author of Whodunit crime novels. He created four series of detective stories: the first one with Reginald De Puyster, a sophisticated detective similar to Philo Vance; the second one with his more famous character, Lieutenant Valcour; Colin Starr, who appeared in four stories in the *Strand Magazine* during 1940/41; and Detective Bill Duggan, who appeared in three stories in 1956/57. The Bill Duggan stories include his most famous short work, "Malice in Wonderland" (which loaned its title to his 1958 hardcover short story collection).

Modern critics are rediscovering Rufus King's work. Mike Grost, on *Golden Age Detective*, features a long writeup of King, stating: "King had a vivid writing style, with colorful characters, events, and images. He was clearly a born writer."

www.ingramcontent.com/pod-product-compliance
Lightning Source LLC
Chambersburg PA
CBHW032205190626
46810CB00018B/1723